Robin Goddard's body wa~~s~~
that the rest of him is or
(both boys); used to live o
setter/collie cross dog cal.__ _____, ...,
motorbike (and has a tattoo to prove it!); and he has
an ex-wife. Oh yes, and he's a lawyer. When you read
the book, you'll understand why all that is relevant –
if not necessarily funny. As they (who *are* 'they'
anyway?) say, the rest is history, biology, geography
and (auto)biography – but mostly fiction!

June Trafford was certainly born – and she used to
have pretensions (with some justification) to being a
Fine Artist. Then she met Robin, who persuaded her
(with 2 halves of 'the black stuff' and a roast dinner if
you must know!) to come over to the 'dark side' –
the, slightly seedy, shadow world of book illustrating.
She has since developed a more hard-headed attitude
to art, life and roast beef.

A VERY ENGLISH BEAR

247 of 250

Written by
Robin Goddard

With illustrations by
June Trafford

pNs
PUBLISHING

A Very English Bear
Robin Goddard

First published in the UK in November 2011 by PNS Publishing

PNS Publishing, Suite 150 Andover House, George Yard, Andover, Hants,
SP10 1PB

ISBN 978-1-908789-00-6

A CIP catalogue for this book is available from the British Library

Cover Design by June Trafford

Printed and bound by Good News Digital Books

Paper stock used is natural, recyclable and made from wood grown in
sustainable forests. The manufacturing processes conform to
environmental regulations.

Thanks to......

Adam for lots of stuff (he knows!) and for U Support.

Bishop Michael for being a great sport and for being ungrown-up.

June for helping rekindle my enthusiasm and for the absolutely *stonking* drawings!

Lettie (RIP) for being waggie and unconditionally great!

Lord Cholmondeley for the name, being a great sport and for being ungrown-up too!

Mary for what was, long ago, actually an Xmas present.

Nigel for tactful objectivity and perspective.

Sandy for loads (more than she knows!), and speshlee cos she sawtid owt mi pungchewashun and spelin.

Sarah for organising Bishop Michael, and general helpfulness!

Simon also for lots (he knows!), but mostly for the intro.

Tracey for keeping Adam grounded.

But mostly this book is for, and is dedicated to:

Alex and Ian – they may be the last names in this list but they are *always* first, jointly, with me.
They are what it is all about and what it is all for.

Robin Goddard
Southampton
November 2011

Become Reggie's friend on
www.facebook.com/ReggiesPage

CHAPTER 1

Reginald Arbuthnot Chumley woke up – and this happened all of a sudden.

"Where am I?" he thought.

He knew he was in a very comfortable bed with his head on a very comfortable pillow, but where was the bed?

Slowly pulling down the covers he peeped, cautiously, over the top. It was dark and a little chilly, so he quickly pulled the covers back up, putting his head back where it was warm and (not that he was scared of course!) safe. Just to be sure though, he closed his eyes tight shut.

He couldn't close his ears (he had tried!) so he could hear what sounded like gently splashing water outside.

His whole self was, little by little, becoming increasingly aware of more unexpected and interesting stuff.

Now, because he was more fully awake, he could feel that the bed was rocking, slowly, from side to side. "Why is that?" he wondered.

As his brain gradually came online he realised what was causing the movement.

"I must be on a boat," he whispered to himself, "what fun!" and he poked his head out again to see what he could see.

A light came on behind him, prompting Reginald Arbuthnot Chumley to pull the quilt over his head again (well, it was the sensible thing to do until he knew a bit more about what was happening – but him, scared, no, never, of course not!).

As his head came up past the top of the quilt (and also past his hands, which were still holding it) he noticed something odd.
"I've got furry hands!!"

The light went out and a somewhat large something 'plonked' itself into the bed next to him and said, "Of course you have, you're furry all over. Go back to sleep Reggie, goodnight."

Without thinking about it, Reginald Arbuthnot Chumley absent-mindedly replied, "Goodnight," lifted the covers high enough to see under them, looked down, and saw, in the dim moonlight, that he was furry all over.

He felt his head (which was, of course, also furry) and, as the truth dawned on him, spluttered, *"Great Gherkins, I'm a Bear! "*

And with that thought, he went back to sleep.

Reginald Arbuthnot Chumley woke up. Not quite as suddenly as the last time - although he was still confused. It might have been a new confusion, but it felt to him very much the same as the confusion in the middle of the night so it doesn't really matter whether it was different or not!

This time there was enough light drifting in lazily through the windows to better make out his surroundings, so he could see that the thing that had so unceremoniously 'plonked' itself next to him during the night was actually a human being with a very hairy face (it was a beard!) who was fast asleep.

Reginald Arbuthnot Chumley looked around. He was in an 'L' shaped room with gently curving walls that was moving smoothly back and forth to the rhythm of the waves lapping against the side of the boat – he did at least remember working out that he was on a boat. Remembering that he had worked that out made him feel slightly better, and slightly less confused.

He looked to his left where he could see an open door, and beyond that, more rooms. This was obviously where he now lived, and, although he was still a bit disorientated, he somehow knew that it would feel like home in no time at all.

In an effort to really get things straight in his head (he didn't like not being in full possession of the facts, or at all confused!) he closed his eyes and started thinking - as hard as he could!

. . . . . . The first thing he could remember was being in a small, cluttered, but oddly not really *that* untidy, shop. "Well, more an emporium." he said to himself, because he liked to be precise about these things.

A female human had brought him to the boat he was now on.

The human had thought she was choosing him as a belated Easter present for a friend, but somehow he knew differently. He just *knew* that he knew that Bears choose their Humans - not the other way round. How he knew that he hadn't worked out yet, but he filed that under 'stuff I can think about later' as it didn't seem important at the moment.

In some way he knew that He had chosen this particular human female because he also knew, intuitively, that she would deliver him to the one who would benefit most from being looked after by a Bear like him.

The human with the beard was clearly the one that had been chosen . . . . . .

"Pickled Walnuts!" he muttered to himself when he recalled that he had a tag on in the shop and that the sales assistant lady had written his name on it. The problem was that she had spelt it as it sounds and not as it should be spelt.

The reason this really worried Reginald Arbuthnot Chumley (spelt as it sounds) was because, in some way he didn't understand yet, he just knew that he was actually Reginald Arbuthnot Cholmondeley (pronounced Chumley), 9th Viscount of the Salop Oak and not just plain Reggie the Bear!

He knew that something would have to done (and really rather soon!) about restoring his proper name and rank, but, being the pragmatist he was, and as there was nothing he could do about that immediately, he decided that he had better find out more about his new circumstances.

Obviously the first item on the agenda was to find out just who his new Human was, so he determined there and then to wake him up and ask.

Waking up the hairy human next to him was not quite as easy as it sounded because Reginald Arbuthnot Chumley was not an enormous Bear and the human with the beard was quite a large specimen who was plainly fast asleep.

Reginald Arbuthnot Chumley, who was a very polite Bear, first tried making "Ahem, ahem" noises – which, quite predictably, had no positive result whatsoever! "Worth trying the polite method first though", he thought to himself.

He then attempted a gentle nudge with his paw against the human's shoulder. He might as well have tried to blow Mount Everest over with a whistle for all the good that did!

"Ah, well, I suppose I have no choice then" he thought aloud. And so, without any more ado, Reginald Arbuthnot Chumley bellowed (there's no other way to describe it) into the human's left ear.

"WOULD YOU MIND AWFULLY WAKING UP."

Then, half a second later, he added "PLEASE," as he was, after all, a well brought up Bear.

This had the desired effect in that it woke the human up. What, however, Reginald Arbuthnot Chumley was not entirely ready for was the extra rocking of the boat and the dreadful "whatwhatwhatwhat" noise that followed.

Reginald Arbuthnot Chumley was also not prepared for the fact that the movement of such a large (relative to the Bear) human close by meant that the amount of available space in the immediate vicinity shrunk very quickly, causing the Bear to tumble, in a most undignified manner, out of the bed and onto the deck below.

"Ooooof!" said Reginald Arbuthnot Chumley.

"What was that?" From the bed came a deep, but kind, voice.

4

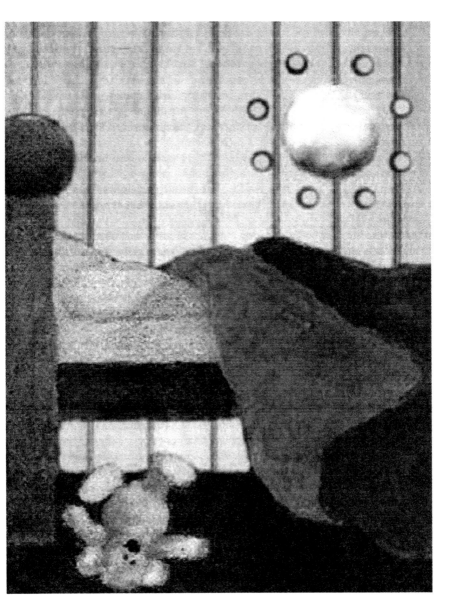

His Human with the beard was awake at last!

"I wonder if you would mind helping me back onto the bed," Reginald Arbuthnot Chumley asked, "it's not exactly comfortable being in a heap on the floor you know."

"Is that you, Reggie? What are you doing down there?"

"You pushed me out!" Reginald Arbuthnot Chumley was not in a very good mood, and things were not going entirely according to plan.

An arm stretched down, picked him up by one leg, and hauled him up, effectively but unceremoniously, onto the pillow.

"Well, thank you very much." muttered Reginald Arbuthnot Chumley as he snuggled himself back down under the quilt. In a vain effort to regain some of his dignity, he said, "I think we had better be formally introduced."

"I am Reginald Arbuthnot Chumley, apparently spelt as it sounds."

He paused, to let this information sink in. Then he went on "But my real name is Reginald Arbuthnot Cholmondeley (which is *pronounced* Chumley), 9th Viscount of the Salop Oak. How do you do?"

"Very well, thank you," said the Human. "My name is Robin Goddard.

I say do you mind if I keep calling you Reggie, your full name's a bit of a mouthful and calling you 'My Lord' or 'Your Lordship' does seem a bit formal in all the circumstances. Anyway, this is my dream so I should be able to do what I like in it."

"The bruise on my bottom isn't a dream," said Reginald Arbuthnot Chumley, crossly, "but I suppose you can call me Reggie, nevertheless."

"If this isn't a dream, then how come you're talking to me like a human being - you're a Teddy Bear?"

"I am not a **TEDDY** Bear," spluttered Reginald Arbuthnot Chumley, indignantly, "they are from the American Colonies. I am a British Bear of ancient, latterly noble, lineage and I'll thank you to remember that in future!"

"Sorry, I'm sure, Reggie that mistake won't happen again."

Reginald Arbuthnot Chumley sighed. This Human was going to be hard work!

"OK then, Reggie, I'm listening - how come you can talk to me?" Robin propped himself up on his elbows and stared intently at the Bear.

If Bears could blush then this one might have done so - but, luckily, they can't, at least on the outside! Instead Reginald Arbuthnot Chumley heaved another Bear sigh and began.

"It has been well known for many generations that all children are quite capable of communicating with Bears. They are also, of course, able to see Fairies, Elves, Gnomes and the like. However, for reasons I am sure I need not explain, they *MUST NOT* attempt to see, hear or talk to Father Christmas, the Tooth Fairy or the Easter Bunny." Reginald Arbuthnot Chumley paused there – for effect!

When this got no response he went on "I assume you know this already?" He said this in a, frankly, sarcastic way (well his bottom was sore and his pride had definitely been hurt as a result of rolling off the bed and onto the floor).

"Go on, go on, this really is great stuff. I don't know where I got the imagination to have a dream like this - it's marvellous! Must have been that slightly past its sell by date stilton I had last night."

Robin plainly thought he was still asleep and so completely ignored the fact that Reginald Arbuthnot Chumley was clearly somewhat miffed with him.

"Aardvarks and Artichokes, this isn't a dream!" groaned the Bear, thinking to himself at the same time, "What did I do to deserve a Human like this one?" He conveniently forgot that he was the one who had chosen the Human!

Reginald Arbuthnot Chumley swallowed hard, counted to three (he wasn't patient enough to go all the way to ten!) and went on. "Listen, Robin, Bears can talk to adults - but only if they aren't actually grown-up."

"You see it's all a matter of belief. Children are born totally innocent and without any preconceptions so they believe that

7

they can converse and otherwise interact with pretty much anything – which means that they can. Grown-ups very rarely believe the truth that children have got it right and they, the grown-ups, have got it wrong – even when it is staring them squarely in the face! In the end, tired of not being believed, most children, sadly, simply stop believing and become grown-up themselves."

He stopped there, waiting for a reaction.

To say the least, Robin did not look convinced. Reginald Arbuthnot Chumley sighed yet again (he was a Bear who did that an awful lot!).

At last Robin decided that he had better say something.

"Are you telling me that I'm not grown-up then?"

This idea seemed to upset him which Reginald Arbuthnot Chumley found rather difficult to understand. Did this Human really want to be grown-up?

The Bear thought for a second and then remarked, somewhat cautiously because this way of looking at things hadn't, until that moment, actually occurred to him, "I suppose you could put it like that. Obviously I can talk to you, and, apparently, you can understand and talk to me. As the clearest indicator of being grown-up is not being able to do that then that must make you not grown-up - I think!

Once again Reginald Arbuthnot Chumley was confused – and this was definitely a new type of confusion.

Just at that moment there was an unutterably hideous clamour.

Reginald Arbuthnot Chumley was almost (but not quite) knocked out of the bed again as Robin threw aside the quilt and leapt over to the clock, saying as he did so, "Oh botheration, I thought I'd left it on radio!"

As Robin frantically began pulling on a tracksuit and grabbing a towel and wash bag he said, "Great dream, Reggie, I even remembered it. Must dash or I'll be late for work."

And with that he disappeared up the steps calling out "Come on Lettie" to something (or someone) that Reggie couldn't see.

Reginald Arbuthnot Chumley watched, speechless, motionless,

and hanging onto such bedclothes as he could grab so as to avoid the utter indignity of falling back onto the deck. About 20 minutes later Robin came back.

He put on a clean, apparently recently

pressed white shirt, the trousers of a smart blue suit (he left the jacket hanging on the wardrobe), highly polished black shoes and a vaguely silly, but exceptionally colourful, bowtie (which he tied himself).

While Robin was doing this he continued talking to Reggie at such a pace that the Bear had absolutely no chance to get a word in - and nothing he said was particularly interesting or at all memorable!

When he was completely dressed Robin bounded out of the bedroom with a jolly "Cheerio, Reggie, see you this evening."

And before Reginald Arbuthnot Chumley could reply, the Human was gone!

After Robin had left the Boat Reginald Arbuthnot Chumley sighed again (he obviously did do that a lot!) and then nearly jumped out of his skin.

A very wet nose was nuzzling him!

Reginald Arbuthnot Chumley slowly moved his head around to see who the perpetrator of this undignified nuzzlement was.

It turned out to be a medium sized, mostly black, dog with little reddish streaky bits and black and white paws.

"Oh! You must be Lettie."

Reginald Arbuthnot Chumley was, it must be said, a very perceptive Bear.

At the mention of her name the Dog wagged her tail furiously and then began licking the Bear's face.

"No, no, no, no, no! Stop that this instant!" Reginald Arbuthnot Chumley was not prepared to let this dog (or, indeed, anyone else!) get away with that sort of behaviour - after all a Bear has standards!

Lettie the Dog pottered off to another part of the Boat, completely oblivious to the fact that she had just committed an enormous social gaffe - at least as far as Reginald Arbuthnot Chumley was concerned! The Dog quite clearly couldn't have cared less!

The radio was playing softly. It appeared that Robin had left it on so that Lettie wouldn't get too lonely whilst he was at work.

Reginald Arbuthnot Chumley settled back in bed and listened to the music for a time while he collected his thoughts, moved them about a bit in his mind and then sorted them out into the order that he wanted.

The 'thought sorting' took him a very long time because there were an awful lot of 'thoughts to think'.

In fact he was so busy sorting out all his thoughts that he missed the noise Lettie made when, a few hours later, Robin came back to take her for a middle of the day walk.

Before Reginald Arbuthnot Chumley knew it the whole day had gone.

This time however, he heard Lettie bounding about in the next room.

Then he heard Robin's voice.

"All right, all right, yes, yes, yes, I've missed you as well girlie, at least let me get on board, eh!"

Robin came into the bedroom. He hung his jacket on a hanger and called out cheerily, "Hello, Reggie, have you had a good day?"

Clearly Robin was not expecting an actual answer from the Bear, who, by now, was leaning nonchalantly against one of the corner posts of the bed.

Robin continued taking off his work clothes, putting them away neatly and organising his rather more comfortable 'being at home on the Boat' clothes.

Reginald Arbuthnot Chumley's day had, in fact, been extremely good. He had filled all the gaps in his memory and he was already beginning to feel at home on the Boat – or, for the moment at least, at home in the bed on the Boat!

Robin obviously did not remember (or more likely had forgotten or just didn't believe) that his Bear had been talking to him that very morning and he was happily chatting away to Reginald Arbuthnot Chumley and Lettie about the sort of day he had had without pausing to allow either of them to answer.

Reginald Arbuthnot Chumley was a Bear with a rather naughty sense of humour. He considered that he was justified still being slightly miffed at having been knocked, abruptly, out of his (he had already started thinking of it as 'his') warm bed in the middle of the night, and felt that Robin needed to be taught consideration for others ('others', in this case, in point of fact only meaning Reginald Arbuthnot Chumley himself!).

This was probably a touch unsporting in the circumstances, as Reginald Arbuthnot Chumley could not honestly expect Robin to know about talking Bears as he was (apparently) a grown-up and therefore not really supposed to understand.

Anyway, whatever the rights or wrongs of the situation, Reginald Arbuthnot Chumley waited until Robin had his trousers half on and half off and then said "Actually I had a very good day. Thank you for asking."

This made Robin stop what he was doing in the middle of the doing of it (which was definitely a big mistake!), look over at the bed, and then (quite gracefully as it happens) fall over in a heap almost exactly like Reggie's had been - except it was a lot bigger!

The expression on Robin's face was priceless and Reginald Arbuthnot Chumley wished he had a camera!

"It wasn't a dream this morning - was it?"

"No, it wasn't."

And that really was all that needed to be said!

Robin got up off the floor and sat down on the bed, his trousers still half on and half off. He leant over to one side and rubbed his bottom. This prompted him to remember what had happened that morning.

"I hope your bottom is better now?"

Robin said this with such obvious concern that Reggie, who wasn't malicious by nature, actually felt quite guilty about the trick he had played because, in all honesty, his bottom hadn't been very bruised at all - it was really only his pride that had been hurt!

"It's much less uncomfortable, thank you."

Robin seemed happy with the answer.

He got up off the bed and finished taking off his trousers and put on the hanger with his jacket.

While he was putting on his 'being at home on the Boat clothes' Robin, trying to sound as if talking to a Bear was something he did every day, remarked, "So, what did you do today?"

Being the perceptive Bear he undoubtedly was, Reginald Arbuthnot Chumley realised that Robin really wanted to ask him lots of questions like: How can you talk to me? Who else can you talk to? Where do you come from? When am I going to wake up? (That one was a very *grown-up* sort of question). Why me? And other similar queries.

Reggie knew that Robin was confused. Evidently he had forgotten everything he had known before he grew up and had shut his believing away inside.

Reggie felt a great wave of sadness flow over him. What a truly frightful thing to do to oneself.

"Is this what all grown-ups do?" he thought sorrowfully.

"Please sit down." Robin did (he was practically dressed by now).

"Are you sitting comfortably?" Robin nodded.

"Then I'll begin."

Before he 'began', Reginald Arbuthnot Chumley made a request.

"I say, Robin, would you, please, be good enough to pass me that smart night-shirt which I believe came with me?"

This was said in what was a most un-Reginald Arbuthnot Chumley type voice. The fact is that he had only just remembered that he didn't have any clothes on — and he was a trifle embarrassed!

"You see, Robin," Reginald Arbuthnot Chumley explained, I am not the sort of Bear who is in the habit of lying around in bed all day, but I felt quite unable to get up because I wasn't dressed at all, and walking around starkers would hardly have been the proper thing to do!"

Robin had been sitting on the bed with his mouth wide open in stunned amazement at what was happening. He closed it with a faint 'plop', leapt to his feet and dashed out of the room.

When he returned, mere seconds later, he was holding the nightshirt.

He reached out and handed it to the Bear.

The Bear gave a

delicate cough, turned his back and said, as he did so, "Would you excuse me, please?"

When Reginald Arbuthnot Chumley was dressed he gave a sigh of pure contentment and remarked not really to anyone in particular, "That is so much better - I feel positively ursine again." He turned back to face Robin. "Now, where were we?"

"You were about to answer all my questions, I hope," said Robin, who had obviously forgotten that he had not actually asked all the questions that Reggie (being as has been said, an insightful Bear) had known he wanted answered.

"Ah, yes." said Reggie, "Are you sitting comf......."

Before he could finish Robin butted in, saying, "You've done that bit. Do get on with it. Please."

Luckily for him he had remembered to add 'please'.

The use of 'please' was only just in time to stop Reginald Arbuthnot Chumley giving him a *look* - which was just as well because the sort of *looks* Bears have are deadly!

Reginald Arbuthnot Chumley was a bit stuck. It had never been necessary to explain the bare Bear facts before because, as far as he knew, Bears always had a Human who understood - at least that was what he remembered being taught.

"Well," he began uncertainly; "You see the thing is this," and then he stopped, as, in all honesty, he was not entirely sure what 'the thing' actually was!

He tried once more, hoping that inspiration would strike before his mouth made his face look silly. Luckily for him his memory came flooding back.

"Bears have been here for an awfully long time. In fact the first recorded Bear having a Human in Britain was in the time of the Vikings, and we were certainly in Viking lands before that. They also went down into Northern France so some then came across to Britain with the Norman Conquest.

Reginald Arbuthnot Chumley paused. He wanted to tell Robin something that might sound like boasting and he wasn't quite sure how to say it.

In the end he decided that the only way was just to blurt it out.

"As a matter of fact that was when my family came here, with William the Conqueror – you know 1066 and All That!"

"There," he thought to himself, "that didn't sound too bad."

He went on. "My ancestor, Regis les Cholmde (pronounced ley Chum), had a Human who was one of Duke William's personal Guards. He was knighted immediately after the Battle of Hastings - for conspicuous valour!"

Robin interrupted at this point, "Who was it that was knighted, your great-great-great-great, oh however many greats it is, grandfather or his human?" Then, realising what he had just said, he added, "And what do you mean by 'his Human', surely it's the other way round?"

Given all the new stuff he was having to process he thought he had better check this, so he added, "Isn't it?"

"My ancestor was knighted, of course." In fact the Human had been knighted too, but Reginald Arbuthnot Chumley didn't feel that now was the best time to admit it!

Reginald Arbuthnot Chumley could be very pompous when he felt anyone was not taking him seriously – and at other times too, but you have probably already realised that.

A note of exasperation crept into Reginald Arbuthnot Chumley's voice. "And haven't you realised yet that *Bears* choose their Humans and not the other way round!"

He went on "Usually we get a Human when he or she is a small child but in your case, I appear to be stuck with a fully grown, adult one!"

At this juncture another Reginald Arbuthnot Chumley sigh was sighed. It seemed a good place for one!

Reginald Arbuthnot Chumley carried on. "Regardless of what you might have thought, Bears have often played a terrifically important, frequently decisive, part in the history of this country - and lots of others come to that!"

Reginald Arbuthnot Chumley began counting on his hand claws.

"The les Cholmde (pronounced ley Chum) family are shown in the Bayeux Tapestry; were the ones who thought of the Domesday Book; took part in the Crusades; showed Robin Hood how to use a longbow; signed Magna Carta (at this point he went onto his other paw); persuaded the Black Prince to wear black armour (it looked so elegant!); mostly survived the Black Death; told Henry V to go 'once more into the breach'; and picked both the red and the white flowers for the Wars of the Roses!"

Reginald Arbuthnot Chumley stopped there because he had run out of claws.

As he bent down to start on his foot claws he said, "By this point in time we'd changed our name to Cholmondeley (*pronounced* Chumley)."

Robin, who was very impressed (despite himself!), found the sight of the Bear bending over incredibly comical and he laughed out loud - not a good move!

Reginald Arbuthnot Chumley unbent slowly and, giving Robin one of his deadliest *looks*, said, very quietly and very coldly, "Excuse me, is something amusing us? Perhaps you would be good enough to share the joke?"

This was said in such a way as to make it quite clear that Robin had better not say anything else - and that stopping laughing would be very sensible!

Robin instantly shut up – he may have still been a bit disorientated but he had a keen sense of self-preservation and he knew that this was the only sensible thing to do!

"As I was saying, before I was so rudely interrupted," Reginald Arbuthnot Chumley went on. He paused, then, recognising that bending over and counting on his feet was not dignified, decided to use his hand claws again.

"Cholmondeleys have been present at, and indeed, responsible for, a great many of the most important events in the history of Britain. There was a Cholmondeley at the court of Henry VIII, who managed to keep his Human's head on all the way through the reign! Francis Cholmondeley helped his Human see off the Spanish Armada - and then sailed with him all the way round the world!"

He paused, as he had reached a point in his narrative where something personally important was about to be divulged.

"In the English Civil War we were, naturally, on the King's side - so much more romantic I always think."

Reginald Arbuthnot Chumley stopped talking for a moment and looked up at Robin to check that he was still listening – and paying attention.

Robin, who, despite clearly being an adult *and* appearing to be grown-up, was actually really quite bright, said, "I had no idea, Reggie, that Bears were *so* very influential. Do, please, carry on, I'm fascinated."

This was exactly the sort of comment that Reginald Arbuthnot Chumley had hoped to hear.

What he didn't notice, it must be said, was that Robin had put his tongue firmly in his cheek when saying it!

"We now come to one of those coincidences of which history is generally made. In late early September 1651 my ancestor, also called Reginald Arbuthnot Cholmondeley, was staying near Boscobel House in Shropshire with his Human. A few days before King Charles II had fought, but lost unfortunately, a battle at nearby Worcester."

"Reginald's Human put him up an oak tree - something about wanting to protect him. Quite unnecessary, but really quite sweet I've always thought."

"As it so happened Charles chose to conceal himself from the beastly Roundheads in the very same tree."

Reginald Arbuthnot Chumley puffed himself up with pride at this stage and carried on.

"Charles was *so* grateful for the company that he gave Reginald a Viscountcy on the spot - creating him Reginald Arbuthnot Cholmondeley, 1st Viscount of the Salop Oak, in the Peerage of England."

Reginald Arbuthnot Chumley stopped there with, it has to be said, the most ludicrous expression on his face - the sort of look a particularly ripe tomato gives you just before you eat it, all puffed up and ready to burst!

The Bear looked at Robin - obviously waiting for something.

Robin, who knew that type of expression, decided that the best (that is to say the safest!) thing to do in the circumstances was to applaud - so he did, perhaps rather more loudly than necessary, but the Bear was happy!

You will remember that he had only very recently received a Reginald Arbuthnot Chumley *look* - and he did not want another!

The demonstration of praise was exactly what Reginald Arbuthnot Chumley expected and his face showed that he heartily approved.

However the expression the Bear's face plainly belied the thoughts going through his head.

"So you see the name on the tag was wrong. Obviously the lady in the shop had only heard my name rather than read it and she wrote in down inaccurately. In the circumstances I am certain that I do not need to tell you that this mistake simply must be rectified AT ONCE!"

A slight note of panic had crept into Reginald Arbuthnot Chumley's voice!

Robin was, by and large, a kindly soul who did not like to see anyone upset. He had completely come to terms with the fact that 'his' Bear considered that Robin was 'his' Human. He had thought the world of Reggie before he knew this so he was only too willing to help the Bear now that he knew the truth – even though he still didn't really understand what all the fuss over a simple spelling mistake was about.

"What do we need to do then?" Robin's question was the obvious one.

"We must get the Royal Family to acknowledge my claim to the title."

Robin was not expecting this. To have a sentient Bear living with him was one thing; but to have a Noble sentient Bear who wished to have an audience with the Royal Family was another thing altogether!

It did, however, go some way towards explaining why Reginald Arbuthnot Chumley was so very concerned about the spelling mistake.

"I see." said Robin, playing for time. "So, Reggie, how do we do that then?"

Reginald Arbuthnot Chumley started one of his *looks*, but changed his mind.

"I don't know. I rather hoped you would. As far as I am aware this hasn't happened before."

"Hang on, Reggie. Before I can do anything to help I've simply got to have some answers."

Only then did Robin realise his *faux pas* and remember his manners "It is OK for me to call you Reggie, isn't it? I hope you don't mind, but your full name's a bit of a mouthful and calling you 'My Lord' or 'Your Lordship' does seem a bit formal in all the circumstances."

Clearly Robin had completely forgotten their earlier conversation (well, he had thought it was a dream!) and the fact that the Bear had already given him permission to be so familiar!

Reginald Arbuthnot Chumley nodded – he was too flustered to actually say anything – and looked at Robin intently, obviously waiting for him to carry on.

Robin was, frankly, almost completely flummoxed. He knew that seeing the Royal Family wasn't going to be the easiest thing in the world, and that he would need a lot more information.

He needed time to think so he did what everyone does when they have no real idea of what to do next – he stalled!

"OK Reggie. For starters, just how do you know so much about your family history, and where you come from?"

Reggie got up and started walking around on the bed.

This flummoxed Robin even more than he already was. "You can walk?"

"Naturally," said a rather baffled Reginald Arbuthnot Chumley, "I simply chose not to earlier as I was not properly dressed - indeed I was not dressed at all!"

"But..........!" Robin felt that this was simply too much.

He was now way past flummoxed and into absolute and utter befuddlement!

The all too obvious fact that his Human had been thrown totally off balance brought forth another Reginald Arbuthnot Chumley sigh. "Oh, well, I suppose I'd better explain."

Robin nodded. "Yes. Please do, Reggie."

"My Father, the 8th Viscount, told me everything about the family. We have a tradition that Fathers pass on the whole history of the Cholmondeley line to their heir. I shall, no doubt, tell mine in due course."

Robin's mouth began a question, but his brain decided not to risk a *look* and stopped it just in time!

"As to where I come from, that is somewhat more complicated. Shall we just say that I come from *somewhere else* and leave it at that?"

Reginald Arbuthnot Chumley's demeanour made it plain that this was all he was prepared to say on the matter. He was not prepared, clearly, to be drawn any further on the subject so Robin decided to drop it - for now.

All the time Reggie and Robin had been talking, Lettie the Dog had been curled up asleep on an old quilt in the wheelhouse of the Boat.

Now she pootled down the length of the Boat and into the Cabin (which as you probably know, is the proper name for a bedroom on a boat) and began wagging her tail (and her bottom too actually!) while she licked Robin's hand.

"Hello girlie. Do you want your tea?"

This was obviously what Lettie wanted as her tail (and bottom!) became even waggier!

"Please excuse us a second Reggie, duty calls."

And with that Robin meandered along the Boat to the Galley (which is what you call the kitchen on a boat) to sort out the Dog's food.

When Robin came back he found Reginald Arbuthnot Chumley in a bit of a muddle. He had been trying to get off the bed, which was rather high - especially for a Bear who was somewhat vertically challenged (and that is being kind!). In other more accurate but less sensitive words he was really quite short – but it was much better not to mention it anywhere in his vicinity!

The problem was quite simple - Reginald Arbuthnot Chumley was stuck!!

"May I help?"

Robin's question was punctuated by a very short (and very, very quiet!) titter!

Reggie was acutely embarrassed by his undignified position. "Yes." You can tell how flustered the situation made Reginald Arbuthnot Chumley because he forgot to say 'Please'.

As he helped Reggie back onto the bed Robin asked, "Shall I make you a ladder, so you can get on and off more easily?"

Reggie was delighted. "That would be splendid, thank you very much Robin." His good humour restored, he thought to himself "Well perhaps this Human isn't so bad after all."

By now Lettie had finished her food and was hovering. She had her own types of look and she was wearing one now.

"I think she wants to go for a walk, Reggie. Would you like to come?"

Reggie's face positively lit up. "That would be grand. Yes, please. I've been stuck in a shop and on this Boat; not that it isn't a very nice Boat you understand; for a frightfully long time and some fresh air would be wonderful."

He paused, realising that he wasn't really dressed for going out at all - let alone at night, in winter!

Robin immediately understood his predicament.

"None of my clothes will fit you but I do have a big, warm scarf that you could wrap up in. It would cover you completely and you can ride in the pocket of my jacket."

"That's acceptable, for now, thank you. But I must make it clear that I cannot be expected to go without clothes for long, nor, indeed, do I require carrying around like a parcel - at least not all the time."

Reginald Arbuthnot Chumley was a Bear who believed in keeping every one of his available options open!

Robin fetched the scarf, helped Reggie package himself up in it and then put his own coat on.

He very carefully helped the Bear into the voluminous side pocket of his jacket, where he stood with just ears, eyes, nose and chin showing – so, his head then!

Calling out "Come on Lettie," Robin picked up a lead and the three disembarked (which means 'get off' in boat language) and went out into the crisp, clear night.

The first thing that Reggie noticed was how cold it was.

It was a nice cold though, the sort that if you are properly wrapped up makes you think about log fires and other, lovely, warming things.

"Welcome to Emsworth, Reggie."

Unfortunately, as Robin said this, he swung his arms around - just missing Reginald Arbuthnot Chumley's head in the process!

"*Plummeting Pomegranates, watch out!*" cried Reginald Arbuthnot Chumley, ducking down into Robin's pocket as he did so. "You almost took my head right off!"

This was a slight exaggeration - because Robin's arm hadn't come close, let alone actually touched him!

Reggie's complaint was very difficult to hear because it was all muffled – but Robin got the general idea!

"Ooops. Sorry, Reggie."

"Well, please be more careful in future," said Reginald Arbuthnot Chumley with a *look* that, fortunately for Robin, was wasted because it was dark!

"Anyway," Robin continued, somewhat lamely, "here we are."

Reggie peered out from the pocket and saw the most fabulous deep dark blue sky with so many stars that he could have kept counting until next Christmas and still not counted them all!

"Gosh!" Reggie was speechless.

"Pretty spectacular, eh!"

Robin never tired of the wonder of looking up at the beauty of the clear night sky. Both Bear and Human suddenly felt very small but at the same time very close to each other.

Robin was the first to break the silence. "I really do think I'm going to like living with a Bear."

Reggie gave him a different sort of look – but this was one that Robin didn't even need to see to feel really very pleased about.

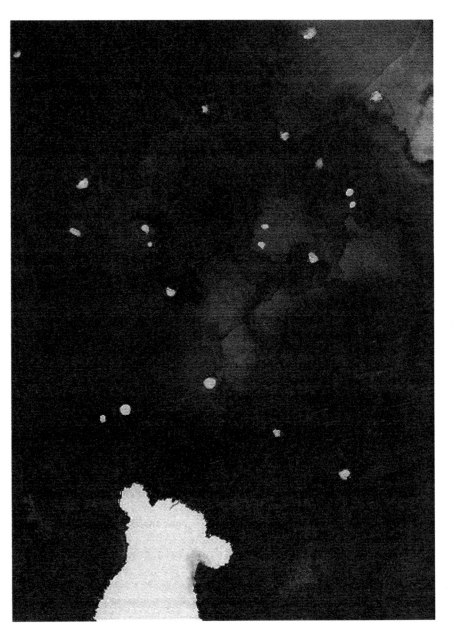

CHAPTER 2

Reginald Arbuthnot Chumley woke up.

This time he knew exactly where, and who, he was. Still asleep beside him was Robin - his Human.

Reggie let out a deep sigh of satisfaction - all was well with the world – and *then* he remembered.

"My Family Name!!"

"Yes, yes, Reggie, but a bit later, eh! There's a good chap. It is Saturday you know!" said a very sleepy voice.

Robin was evidently still on automatic pilot as he asked, "What time is it anyway?"

"It appears to be half past six - time we were getting up and doing."

"Now listen, Reggie." Robin tried his stern voice. Sometimes it actually even worked – but this was not one of those times!

"Yes?" Reginald Arbuthnot Chumley used the verbal equivalent of a *look*!

Undeterred, Robin carried on, "Look here Reggie, I work jolly hard all week, surely I'm entitled to a little peace and quiet on a Saturday morning - at least until seven o'clock?"

"Oh please come on, do. Time's a wasting. We've got my title to get sorted."

Reginald Arbuthnot Chumley was not going to be swayed from his intended course, and Robin wasn't alert enough to stand a chance!

"OK, fine, Reggie. What do we do first then?"

"We visit the Library to check out who's who in What's What."

"The Library!!" Robin was definitely not amused. "It doesn't open until ten!!"

Reginald Arbuthnot Chumley wisely decided that discretion was the better part of valour - and disappeared back under the covers.

Some time later Robin reluctantly allowed Reggie to persuade him, finally, to get out of bed.

"Before we can do anything else," (Robin was clearly determined to have some say in what was going on!) "I must feed and walk the Dog, wash and dress - not necessarily in that order."

"Certainly." said Reginald Arbuthnot Chumley, "One must always look after one's animals and other dependants first."

Robin had the distinct feeling that he wasn't in control at all!

"I would also be most grateful if you could find me some clothes."

Any lingering ideas that Robin may have clung to about being in command of the situation evaporated as Reginald Arbuthnot Chumley reminded him that well brought up Bears do not wander around in their nightshirts!

"All right, Reggie, that's next on my list," said Robin, capitulating as gracefully as he could in the circumstances while he helped the Bear down off the bed.

Robin took Lettie with him to the showers. It being the weekend Robin could take longer than usual to do his ablutions - and he planned to take all the time he could to make sure he was completely awake!

Reginald Arbuthnot Chumley, who was obliged, in the absence of any clothes except his nightshirt, to wait on the Boat, took the opportunity to have a good nose about.

Reginald Arbuthnot Chumley had a good look around the Cabin, which doubled as a sort of study come comfy chilling out area. As

27

well as the double bed it had what looked like a very cosy looking armchair and a desk (actually a big board propped across two chests of drawers) with a laptop and lots of papers on (think 'organised chaos!).

On the desk (which Reggie got to by climbing on the chair, somewhat inelegantly – luckily there was no one there to see!) he found some papers relating to the vessel.

He discovered that she was a Luxe Motor Dutch Barge, originally built in 1933, and that her name was 'ALEXIAN'.

He also found out that she (boats are always called 'she') was 20 metres long (which Reggie calculated to be 65 feet in what he considered to be 'proper' dimensions!), 4 metres (about 13 feet) wide and 1.85 metres (just over 6 feet) high inside at her tallest.

While Reginald Arbuthnot Chumley was 'exploring', Robin came back all fresh and clean and raring to go.

"Hello Reggie, have you been having a good old nose about?"

This, of course, was precisely what Reginald Arbuthnot Chumley had been doing, but to admit it would not have been dignified so he confined his reply to merely saying, "Err...... yes actually, very interesting."

The sight of Reggie at a loss was quite entertaining - but Robin, sensibly, decided not to comment. After all it isn't kind to take advantage of someone's embarrassment - even if it is funny!

"Right then, Reggie, let's find you some apparel consistent with your station – or, failing that, something comfy and warm at least."

"My Father, the 8th Viscount, was always dressed by his Savile Row Tailor, but I understand she no longer operates from there."

Robin had been about to point out that bespoke clothes were likely to be outside his budget when he remembered something or, more correctly, someone.

"My friend Barbara used to be a Master Tailor - well a Mistress Tailor, I suppose. She lives here in the village."

He thought for a moment, and then said, "I'm sure she'd help."

"Splendid! Drop me off with her for a fitting and you can go to the Library to research the information you say you need."

Things were, yet again, moving a touch quicker than Robin felt he could comfortably cope with so he tried to slow them down.

"Hang on Reggie, let me check with Barbara first. She may not be making clothes now."

This last bit wasn't strictly true because Robin knew very well that his friend did, occasionally, still undertake special commissions. As you can probably guess, what actually made Robin nervous was how he was going to explain that he needed some clothes for a walking, talking Bear!

Totally oblivious to Robin's dilemma, Reginald Arbuthnot Chumley said, "Where are my manners, naturally you must ask this good lady first. I don't know what I was thinking of."

Robin, still desperately trying to work out how to broach the subject with Barbara, replied, "Right, Breakfast first, telephone call after. OK?"

Much to Robin's relief this suggestion found favour with the Bear. "Excellent idea. Hot buttered toast?"

No problem. I happen to have some homemade jam. How does that sound?"

"Homemade jam, eh? Sounds simply scrumptious. Lead me to it."

Robin had no idea how much hot buttered toast with homemade raspberry jam a small (he made *quite* sure he wasn't looking at Reginald Arbuthnot Chumley when he thought *that* bit!) Bear could put away.

As it happened it turned out to be.... well let's just say 'lots' and leave it at that!

Anyway, after a meal consisting of a great many pieces of hot, buttered and jammed toast ("A Bear gets hungry, you know!") and copious amounts of hot sweet tea, Reginald Arbuthnot Chumley sat back and said, "Right, let's get on with it."

Robin had, while eating and drinking, worked out the best method of broaching the subject of his friend making the Bear some clothes. He picked up his mobile telephone (they were, after all, on a boat) and dialled.

"Hello, Barbara, how are you?"

Following a short conversation about each other's health and the weather, Robin got to the point.

"I've a friend staying whose Father used to have his clothes made in Savile Row. You may know him, Reginald Arbuthnot Cholmondeley, 9th Viscount of the Salop Oak."

Robin both spelt and pronounced it properly of course!

Reginald Arbuthnot Chumley heard a charming laugh coming down the telephone, followed by a bit that he couldn't quite catch.

"Well, yes, actually – and he's only got a night-shirt at the moment!"

Barbara obviously replied at some length, as Robin said nothing and just listened for a while.

Eventually Reginald Arbuthnot Chumley simply couldn't restrain his curiosity any more. He nudged Robin and muttered, "What is she saying?"

"Excuse me just a second Barbara, the 9th Viscount is rather anxious to know what is going on." Robin's voice had a distinctly whimsical note to it.

"We're in luck. She was your Father's Tailor and remembers him with great fondness. She would be delighted to meet you to discuss all your sartorial requirements."

Reggie beamed. "Do, please, thank her, and say that I look forward to meeting her as well."

Robin duly relayed this message and finished the conversation with a cheery "See you in about 20 minutes then."

"Right, Reggie, let's see if we can find you something to wear to Barbara's house." He paused, " Do you need shoes?"

The Bear shook his head, "No, my paws are well padded thank you."

Robin went into the Saloon and rummaged about. He came back with a tracksuit, small by human standards, but, as it turned out, large for a Bear.

"This should do. He's about your size. I can't understand why I didn't think of it before."

"Who is 'he'?" asked Reggie, as he began putting on the, far too large, top and bottom.

"Goodness me, in all the fuss and excitement I haven't told you about my two children have I?"

"In point of fact Robin, I don't know much about you at all."

"Well," began Robin, "Are you sitting comfortably?"

He just couldn't resist doing to the Bear what the Bear had just done to him.

Sure enough, Reginald Arbuthnot Chumley rose to the bait. "We haven't got time for all that, just give me an outline for now, please."

"OK Reggie, keep your paws on!"

Reginald Arbuthnot Chumley chose to ignore the slight affront to his pride. He had by now got dressed and had tried (but failed completely) to make the tracksuit fit.

Robin continued. "I've got two children; Alex, who's ten and two thirds, and Ian, who's nine and one third. They currently live in my old house with their mother. The truth is that we are divorced. When we've got everything is sorted then we are going to tell them exactly what has happened, but for the moment they just know that Mummy and Daddy aren't living together any more."

At this point Robin paused, and a slightly sad look passed across his face before he started again.

"I only get to see them at weekends or when I can take a holiday. Today they're off doing something with friends, but they're both coming down to the Boat tomorrow morning for the day so they can meet you then."

Robin paused, then said, somewhat nervously, "Oh, yes, and I'm a lawyer."

"Oh!" said Reggie, "Lawyers are supposed to be terribly grown-up, aren't they? I'm glad to say the Family hasn't had much to do with them over the years."

Robin looked rather sheepishly down at his feet.

"Actually I always thought I was grown-up - until I met you. Now I'm really glad I'm not."

"Well," Reggie said, "you would certainly seem to be in a good profession to help sort out my title."

Robin brightened up at the thought of being useful to his new friend. "Yes, well maybe, let's get on with it then."

As they were getting ready to go a thought struck Robin.

"Reggie. I've seen you moving about - can everyone see you?"

"Well, yes," said the Bear, "everyone can see me move - but not everyone believes it. Grown-ups see but their heads make them flatly refuse to believe it and they just pretend it isn't happening. I'm sure that, as a lawyer, you come across a lot of people who simply deny what is actually as plain as the noses on their faces?"

"Well, now that you come to mention it," Robin replied, "I do - all the time."

Picking up Lettie's lead (which made her go fairly potty because she knew *exactly* what *that* meant – 'walkies') Robin said "She's really good but, to be on the safe side, I always put her on her lead when we get anywhere near to roads and stuff."

Unlocking and opening the door to the outside, Robin got off the Boat by simply stepping across the gap between it and the shore.

He turned round and offered Reggie a hand to help him disembark as the gap was a little wide for him to get over easily.

Reginald Arbuthnot Chumley was on the verge of saying, "I can manage perfectly well, thank you very much," in what would have been a rather sarcastic and mean-spirited way. Luckily, before he could do that, a little voice inside told him that Robin was only being helpful and actually, nice – so it would have been, at best, churlish or at the worst, positively nasty to fling the offer back in his face.

Consequently he took the hand he was offered and jumped from the Boat onto the shore.

As Reggie was jumping (while holding Robin's hand) he became painfully (well fortuitously, *not* painful as such!) aware that he definitely might not have managed to do it on his own – and that he would have fallen into the water!

"Hmmmm, must remember that," he thought, as he noted that Robin had just stepped across and Lettie had sort of 'bounded'

They all started away from the Boat in the direction of the marina gates – Robin walking (at what he genuinely believed to be a Bear's pace) with Reggie alternating between almost jogging and almost trotting!

In all honesty Robin felt just a little self-conscious to be walking along outside with a Bear - especially one who was so obviously enthused by the whole experience.

Reggie kept up a non-stop commentary on everything he saw ranging from "Goodness me, what a lot of boats," (a general remark) to "Well I never, who would dare to be seen out in something that colour!" (a more specific and definitely a more personal observation).

One thing, however, was certainly evident - not one other person paid the slightest attention to the fact that a Bear was walking around on its own and chattering away twenty-three to the dozen.

After a while Reggie asked if they could stop to let him catch his breath. "After all I haven't had much exercise since I came here and...," he paused, obviously uncertain whether to admit to being less than perfect, "well, my legs aren't quite as long as yours are you know!"

Robin took the hint and didn't mention the 'challengedness' of his furry companion in the height department!

"What say we ask Lettie if she'll let you ride on her for a while?"

"Wellllllll," the Bear wasn't sure about this, but he was a bit out of breath and didn't relish carrying on like that, "All right then."

Reginald Arbuthnot Chumley was torn between acknowledging a weakness and the idea (which, as a matter of fact, he thought would be jolly good fun) of travelling in style on Lettie's back, which he thought would be rather like a maharajah riding on an elephant – but scaled down a bit!

It would also avoid the undignified displays of panting which Reginald Arbuthnot Chumley knew were on the cards, as he really was not very fit!

"Come here girlie," called Robin.

Lettie, who was very obedient for a dog with such an enormous sense of curiosity, came ambling back to where Bear and Human waited.

Robin made an adjustment to the Dog's collar and whispered in her ear. With his newly rediscovered sense of reality as it *really* is he could have sworn that Lettie nodded. She certainly wagged her tail but, as she did this an awful lot, Robin discounted it as a part of her answer.

Whether Lettie had responded deliberately or not, she was apparently happy to let the Bear sit on her back. The sleek black Dog stood patiently while Reggie clambered up, huffing and puffing and generally scrabbling inelegantly.

Robin considered offering a helping hand, then decided not to when he remembered how independent his new friend was - but he did put the lead on, even though they were still in the Marina, just to be on the safe side!

Eventually, when he was sitting relatively comfortably on Lettie's back and holding onto her collar, he felt confident enough to let her move, so he said, "Right! Off we go then." He tried to sound self-assured – but failed utterly!

And off they went.

As they came into the town, up the hill and round the corner, Robin pointed up the street. "There it is Reggie, *chez* Barbara."

Then, while they were ambling towards the tall exquisite old townhouse somebody did notice the trio.

A small human female sitting outside a shop on the other side of the road, grinned, waved, giggled, and waved again - saying to her canine companion as she did so "Look over there, Henry, a Bear on a Dog!"

From inside the house a rather grumpy adult voice answered her
(even though she wasn't talking to him at all!) with "Don't be
silly, Lou, come in now." The little girl got up sadly and
disappeared.

"Was I like that?" Robin said to nothing and no one in particular.
"Gosh! Maybe I still am - what do you think Reggie?"

"*Galloping Grapefruit,*" said Reginald Arbuthnot Chumley (who obviously hadn't noticed what had happened) "Have you been listening to me at all Robin? I've done nothing but tell you what I think since we left the Boat!"

Wisely, Robin decided to keep quiet - but he filed the incident away in the 'do not forget this' section of his brain and made a mental note not to ignore his children in future when they told him that they saw something like that.

Robin was un-growing up at last!

When they got to their destination, Robin knocked twice on the big brass knocker. Well, it was a tad high for Reggie!

Lettie's tail and bottom were wagging faster by the second – she plainly recognised where she was and approved! Consequently, as the door opened, the Dog 'bounced' (there is simply no other word for it) in, and the 9th Viscount found himself doing an impromptu rodeo act. Fortunately (he never knew how) Reginald Arbuthnot Chumley managed to stay on - falling off would just have been the absolute end!

Lettie was getting even waggier and was furiously licking the hand of the petite dark haired lady who had opened the door.

"Hello, hello. Yes Lettice (clearly a pet name), I'm pleased to see you as well."

Happy with this, Lettie promptly went off in the direction of elsewhere!

This entirely unforeseen wandering by the Dog caused Reginald Arbuthnot Chumley to lose his balance and, for a moment, he looked certain to tumble gracelessly onto the floor – again!

Fortunately for Reggie Barbara, for this was she, showed great presence of mind as, before he fell off and without any apparent effort, she whisked the Bear from the Dog's back and onto a comfy armchair, which had, or so it seemed, been put there solely for the use of noble Bears!

"Good morning, you must be Reginald. I'm Barbara," she said, "and very pleased I am to meet you. Your Father and I were great friends and I'm sure we will be too."

Robin said, under his breath, "Humans, Dogs and Bears – Quite definitely not in that order. Humphh!!"

"Now, where are my manners? Can I get you something? Tea, biscuits, cake, mince pies – all four?"

This was, rather pointedly apparently directed to the Bear alone - but there was a definite twinkle in her eye as she said it! Before either of her visitors could react Barbara laughed and turning to Robin, gaily planted kisses on both his cheeks.

"Robin, darling, he's exactly what I expected and unsurprisingly, just like his Father, an absolute poppet! You are lucky!"

Robin had long since suspected his friend of being thirty nine, going on fourteen and a half - this clinched it!

Ten minutes later when Reggie and Robin were snugly ensconced contentedly nursing hot drinks and mince pies left over from Christmas, Barbara began the serious business of planning appropriate clothing for the Viscount - she was certainly in no doubt as to his antecedents.

Barbara was displaying various materials and talking to Reggie in 'tailorspeak'.

Robin was gradually losing what little grip he had left on consciousness (he had been woken up rather early after all!) and Reginald Arbuthnot Chumley was taking a keen interest in what the, by now very business like, lady sitting opposite was showing him. She was evidently an accomplished and expert tailor – in short a Master Tailor ("Or *is* that Mistress?" Reggie didn't want to disturb the flow to ask what he was worried might be considered a stupid question!).

Just then Lettie made a re-entrance. She made a beeline straight for Robin and woke him up by the simple but very effective device of licking his hand.

"Right, OK, Yes! What?"

When he realised which planet he was on, Robin said, "I'll go to the library then shall I?"

Although Robin's face was saying "Tell me it's fine if I just drop off again for forty (or sixty two) winks," neither Barbara nor Reggie was really listening. In reply Reginald Arbuthnot Chumley just said, "Yes, good idea."

While Reggie's absent-minded response was not actually what Robin wanted to hear, it was not entirely unexpected.

"Right, I'm off then."

Robin's attempt to get someone to persuade him to stay didn't work - so he got up and got his coat.

"I'll see you later then."

And so saying he completely ignored the unspoken pleas for him to stay, walked over to the front door, opened it and left!

Just over two hours later Robin was outside the door knocking on the brass doorknocker again. It took quite some time for the door to be opened this time. Lettie was standing there being waggy - as usual – but Barbara and Reggie had been so totally absorbed in the task at hand that the former had hardly taken time to draw breath to get up to let Robin in!

Unsurprised at this, Robin went into the kitchen, made himself coffee, came back into the sitting room, sat down - and promptly went off to sleep - again!

The next thing he knew a furry paw was tapping him on the knee.

"What do you think of this, Robin?"

Reginald Arbuthnot Chumley was standing there looking particularly dapper in an off white linen shirt; a dark green tie it yourself bow tie with white spots; and dark green moleskin trousers. This was topped off by a very smart, plain taupe, Bear sized, tweed hacking jacket.

Although not apparent (it was hidden by the jacket) he also had a creamy yellow, brushed velvet waistcoat.

The entire *ensemble* was superb and suited Reginald Arbuthnot Chumley like a dream - but it was held together with pins!

Rubbing his eyes to get rid of the sleep, Robin tried to focus.

Eventually he gave up and said, "Simply splendid, suits you perfectly."

Actually he only said this to give him time to get his eyes matched up with his brain and mouth. When they did and he looked at the outfit properly, Robin was stunned.

"You're better dressed than me!"

"Does Barbara do your clothes?"

Robin shook his head.

"No - then why should you be surprised?"

Robin gave the Bear a taste of his own form of a look (which had no visible effect!) and turned to Barbara.

"OK Barbie," he said, "I know you're a witch but how did you make these things so quickly?"

"Measuring in advance dear boy - forward planning."

Robin looked blank.

"I was there when Reginald made his choices - and I took some details then. I knew he'd need clothes in a hurry - his Father was the same."

She went on, "All I had to do was make a few adjustments - I can finish off everything this afternoon."

Reggie had been staring at Barbara ever since Robin had called her a witch. "Are you really, well, you know, a......"

Before he could finish Barbara said, "A witch? No, of course not, it's a joke between Robin and I that he's a magician and I'm a witch - we're always trying to surprise each other with how quickly we can make things happen."

Reggie looked unconvinced - especially as he didn't actually remember anyone taking his 'details'!

Then he caught a glimpse of himself in the large, floor to ceiling mirror on the wall next to him. "Wow, this really is the business Barbie!"

Realising that this wasn't exactly the sort of comment a Viscount is supposed to come out with he looked down at the floor and shuffled his feet – to the, not exactly hidden, accompaniment of almost, but not quite, furtive titters from both the other two in the room!

In order to relieve some of his friend's obvious embarrassment Robin forced himself to stop tittering and start talking about what he had found out at the Library - after all that had been his task that morning!

"Apparently the Cholmondeley (pronounced as we all know, Chumley) family have been Viscounts since the mid-17th century; but no book I looked in has any real information other than that one single fact - lots of speculation though."

Before he could continue with the results of his researches Reginald Arbuthnot Chumley butted in.

"Are you saying that you doubt the word of a Cholmondeley?" he spluttered.

Robin's plan (for such it was!) to restore the Bear equilibrium level to normal had worked - even though he suffered a *look* as a consequence!

Buoyed up by his newly found confidence however, Robin was unfazed by the Bear's withering gaze. Boldly (and if you've ever had a *look* from a Bear you'll understand what I mean) he carried on. "Listen, Reggie, you asked, nay begged me to go to the Library to check out the position on your family and your title. All

I'm doing is telling you what I found. I didn't, and don't, doubt you for a millisecond!"

Robin's response gave the Bear pause to think!

"You're absolutely right Robin, I apologise."

Once again Reggie found himself having to revise his opinion of his Human – and unquestionably for the better!

"OK, Robin if that's what we've found out then that's what we've got to go on. Where do you go from here?"

Robin started to say, "So, where did the *we* come from – and where did it go when you started talking about action? "

Fortunately for him, Barbara, who was far from silly, spoke first, "What's the problem?" she asked.

Reginald Arbuthnot Chumley began explaining about the mistake made by the lady in the shop; only to be stopped by Barbara (who hadn't been the recipient of a *look* yet – but she was the sort of person who probably wouldn't be fazed by one anyway!) stopped the Bear in mid-explain!

"That doesn't matter you silly goose!" she said.

This clearly unexpected interruption stopped the Bear in his tracks but amazingly, didn't get the normal treatment.

Instead Reginald Arbuthnot Chumley stopped what he was saying and put on a 'listening' face - much to Robin's astonishment! He also made a mental note – which he hoped would help him in the future!

Barbara carried on, "Clearly, once a Viscount, always a Viscount. If you are Reginald Arbuthnot Cholmondeley, the rightful 9th Viscount of the Salop Oak - which no-one here doubts you are," her sideways glance at Robin elicited a rapid head nodding, "then that is who you are - and nothing can change it."

This was said with such conviction that Reginald Arbuthnot Cholmondeley (the power of the confidence of his friends' belief in him kick started his automatic use of the proper spelling again – despite what it had said on the tag!) let his mouth fall open - he was speechless!

"So what do we do about my title and all that, then?" he said when he finally managed to get his mouth working again!

Robin was seeing Reginald Arbuthnot Cholmondeley in a completely new light.

This Bear was a Bear confused - not the positive, self-confident member of the British Nobility who had entered his life - goodness, was it only yesterday – changing (re-changing?) it out of all recognition?

"I'm sorry to ask, Reggie - but why is it so very important?" the no longer completely grown-up Human enquired, his voice expressing the sympathy he felt for his friend.

"It's the last thing that my Father asked me to do – to promise that I would make sure I keep the family's position, title and name alive and functioning - and of course I promised him that I'd do it."

"I see," said Robin, "that explains everything. Well naturally you must keep your promise."

Barbara, who had obviously never grown up anyway and so wasn't having the sort of adjustment problems Robin was, had been thinking.

"Robin," she started questioningly, "what exactly did you find out? Maybe there's something which will help us to help Reginald keep his word."

"You know what, I do believe there is." said Robin. "Right, let me see. Ah! Yes, here we are."

He opened the little black notebook he always carried (when he could remember which coat he'd left it in last time!) and started talking and reading. When Robin managed, eventually, to get his reading and talking in the right order, his audience leaned forward on the edge of their seats waiting for  the pearls of wisdom they were confidently expecting to pour forth. "OK, this branch of the Cholmondeley family, which I believe is yours, first appears, as I said, in the reference books as

Viscounts in the middle of the seventeenth century – which fits of course. The fact that there is a Cholmondeley who is Viscount of the Salop Oak is pretty much the only fact - indeed the actual date of the relevant bit of paper with the Royal doodahs on it even seems to be a bit hazy!

"Royal doodahs! " spluttered Barbara and Reginald Arbuthnot Cholmondeley at the same time, appalled at such *lese majeste*.

"Oh, you know what I mean - signature, royal seal, letters patent, ribbons, bows - all that sort of thing!" Robin was rather taken aback by the stereo onslaught his "doodahs" had brought forth from his two friends!

"Anyway," he said, trying to recover, " there simply aren't any more actual facts about this branch of the Cholmondeleys - no note of a family seat, exploits, hobbies, clubs, charities supported or anything like that.

Now What's What Now's entry is so small I wrote the whole thing down in full and I quote."

Robin looked down at his notebook again and read from it.

"CHOLMONDELEY (pronounced Chumley), hereditary Viscounts of the Salop Oak in the Peerage of England. Created by Charles II. Patent misplaced. Whereabouts or existence of current incumbent of title (presumed 9th Viscount) unknown."

Robin let this sink in for a moment and then carried on. "Then I looked in 'What Was What'. That only had a very small piece about the family that amounted to pretty much the same thing. Oddly enough all the other great families had notes about portraits – who painted which family member, when they did it and where the pictures are now. All that kind of stuff. They even have photographs of some of the more modern people. The entry for the relevant Cholmondeley family had nothing like that whatsoever." Robin paused for effect, looked meaningfully at the Bear and said, "It seems, Reggie, that your family have never had any pictures done of them - ever!"

"Well, OK then." Barbara was the first of the two listeners to recover her composure after this bombshell had been dropped, "Obviously the Bear Cholmondeley family like privacy - or perhaps all the portraits are hidden away in the family vaults."

Reginald Arbuthnot Cholmondeley nodded at this idea, managing to look relieved at the same time!

"That's quite a good theory but...."

Robin paused for effect and then carried on, "no mention of any family vaults in any book and not even any mention of any family houses to have family vaults in – sorry!"

Actually Robin hadn't let the pause be long enough to actually seem like one so the effect was not really significant - although he was quite chuffed that he appeared to have ruffled the *sang froid* of both his friends. Anyway *he* knew he'd paused and that was enough.

"Right." Robin decided to make an effort to take charge of proceedings - after all this might be his only chance! "Undoubtedly an ingenious, not to say crafty, plan is required. What I suggest is this."

This time his pause was a real one, quite clearly noticeable and redolent with meaning – although what that meaning was had yet to be revealed!

Anyway the effect was, for Robin at least, most satisfying, as Barbara and the Bear both leaned even further forward eagerly awaiting his next words.

While Robin outlined his crafty plan Barbara and Reggie sat there, both of them agog, and getting more 'agogger' with each minute.

Occasionally one or other of them would make a quiet comment along the lines of "whoa, that's simply brilliant!" or "splendid wheeze, let's go for it!"

There was, it must be said, one point during the proceedings when Reginald Arbuthnot Cholmondeley let out what can only be described as a 'huff of no confidence' (he actually muttered "balderdash" but luckily no one actually heard the word), which gave the Human a chance to get his own back on the Bear a bit.

Robin stopped abruptly. Barbara and he looked at Reggie as if he was a complete idiot.

Reggie quickly realised that his opinion was both ill considered and in a minority of one and hastily muttered "Sorry. Do, please, carry on. Absolutely marvellous don't you know.........."

The rest of Reggie's mumbled retraction was lost as, while he was muttering, he was also gradually tilting his head forward so that eventually, his face was nearly on his chest; at which point nobody else could hear what he was saying!

This was probably just as well because what he said once he was sure he was safe from being heard was not entirely complimentary!

The last bit, the bit that no one else could hear was, it should be said, more from an unjustified sense of righteous indignation than for any other proper or justifiable reason

Undaunted, Robin carried on describing his plan - to the great relief of the much embarrassed 9th Viscount who realised what a complete idiot he had been about to be!

Eventually Robin finished his explanation and looked expectantly at his audience.

"OK, so what does anyone think?" After what he viewed as almost Herculean efforts, Robin was looking for some validation – and was in desperate need of more tea and cake!

"Well, it is a smidge complicated," said Barbara, "but on balance I think it will work and we haven't got anything else. I vote Yes."

Reginald Arbuthnot Cholmondeley was somewhat less than enthusiastic. "It seems to me that this plan is going to take an awfully long time to come to fruition."

This was met with an acerbic "Oh, really and do you have a better or indeed *any* other ideas?" from Robin who, rightly, was a tad miffed at this.

Reggie, who was fundamentally a fair Bear, answered by saying, "No Robin, I haven't. Sorry to have been negative after all your hard work. Right, I'm in, let's do it!" and with the decision made he put himself four square behind the plan, committed to helping make it succeed.

CHAPTER 3

Reginald Arbuthnot Cholmondeley woke up very early on the day *after* he had met Robin's two Boys for the first time.

This time he was not confused; in fact, given what came into his mind about all the positive things that had happened in such a short space of time, he was suffused with a buoyant, optimistic spirit – which can really only be described as a lovely warm and fuzzy feeling!

With an overwhelming sense of *joie de vivre* he indulged in the luxury of a really big stretching of the arms – the sort of stretch that reaches all the way down to the toes!

"Today's the day we start on getting my name sorted," he said out loud (and quite loudly!) to no one in particular – but in his head he was making an announcement to the whole wide world! This was the sort of scene setting proclamation that would have gone straight into a big production number in any Hollywood / West End / Broadway Musical; but the only response he got was "Gerroffoutofitstillsleepynottimetowakeupyet!" from what can only be described as a chaotic, though comfy, pile of bedclothes.

Under these was Robin – and he was very unimpressed at being almost woken up far too early on a workday!

Reggie was unrepentant. He was in far too good a mood to allow the barely comprehensible whinges of his half-awake Human faze him, or puncture his cheerfulness.

Nonetheless he realised that he had responsibilities towards Robin and that one of these was to let him get his rest – provided of course that there wasn't stuff to be done that the Bear considered important to do!

It was, he was prepared to concede, too early to actually do anything towards the 'crafty plan' for getting his name and title back, so he resolved to get snug again - then have a good think!

After about twelve and a half seconds however, Reggie was forced to acknowledge that while snug was great, it wasn't exactly what he wanted just then – he was in the mood for some action!

He then thought through the ramifications of this and with a huge dollop of honesty changed it to "Well, maybe not *action* as such."

Just to buff out the dent to his self-esteem the Bear decided to settle on "Just not *inaction*, no matter how cosy that might be!"

Having justified things to his own satisfaction (a useful talent for a Bear with high standards!) Reginald Arbuthnot Cholmondeley set about considering what he *could* do within the parameters he had set himself.

Basically he realised that he was in danger of being bored – and he needed to deal with the situation before it became a problem! "I know, I'll tidy the Boat; that will give me something to do and will also please Robin."

Satisfied with his solution (which reset the 'imminent boredom' alarm in his head) the Bear slid out from under the duvet and moved down the bed to where 'his' (well *he* thought of it as that) new ladder was lashed on to stop it falling down.

As he climbed rather gingerly (he wasn't completely used to it yet!) down the rungs he thought about what had happened the day before (which, so you won't get confused, was Sunday).

This had been the day he had met Robin's Boys for the first time, when they had come to spend the day on the Boat with their Father.

This was also going to be the day that they were to meet Reggie and he to meet them – for the very first time!

CHAPTER 3 ½

. . . . . . Reginald Arbuthnot Cholmondeley had woken up quite early on Saturday morning.

Robin was already up and doing stuff. As he hadn't been disturbed, Reggie assumed Robin had got out of bed carefully so as not to disturb him – which was, as it turned out, true.

It was clear that Robin had indulged in a comprehensive bout of 'shipshaping' (which is apparently the proper term for making things neat on a boat) because, when he finally did wake up, Reggie could not fail to notice how 'shipshape' things were.

In fact Robin *had* been considerate when doing his chores, but actually Reggie was sleeping so soundly (and yes, he snores!) he needn't have bothered!

It appeared that after doing all that needed doing inside the Boat, Robin had taken Lettie for a walk and done his morning ablutions – because when Reggie finally made a stab at 'awake', Robin was already dressed and generally pottering about in the Cabin and Lettie was eating her breakfast.

Reggie could see her through the Cabin door (he could also hear her – "Not the world's quietest eater, that Dog") and Robin had told him that, on weekdays, Lettie was usually only given food after her walk.

"Morning Robin"

"How dee dodee Reggie. Sleep well?" Robin was obviously in an extremely happy frame of mind!

"Do you know what, I really did". Reggie realised as he said this that he actually had slept particularly well and that he felt oddly more awake than he had at first believed he would.

"Must be the sea air," said Robin, "and the comfortable bed."

Suddenly Robin turned all business like. "Right, the Boys will be here soon so I need you up and doing, spic and span and ready to receive boarders – though not to repel them of course!"

Reggie may have been awake, but while he was quite happy with the concept of 'up' the idea of 'doing' was not really for him just at that moment.

"Give me a chance," he said, "I've only just come to".

Robin grimaced.

While it was nice to have the Bear on the back foot for a change (he already knew that this was not the sort of opportunity to be squandered!) he evidently had more important things to worry about. "No time to waste Reggie. I want you to make a good impression. Our visitors are the most important people in my world and I want, no scrub that, *need* them to like you!"

This was a facet of his human's character that Reggie hadn't seen yet – at one and the same time both very serious and yet somehow also rather vulnerable.

In addition he appreciated that this was, for Robin, a matter of exceptional importance so he made up his mind to do whatever was required.

"No problem" he thought. "Time for me to stand up and be counted."

So he did – stand up that is!

"The kettle has only just boiled so the water should still be hot enough for you to have a wash in the sink." Robin was in 'command' mode and Reggie found himself strangely unable to do anything other than to obey – definitely a new, not especially appealing, sensation for him!

In an effort to get back some of his rapidly fading composure he asked to be helped off the bed as there was still no ladder and it remained rather high for a Bear of his stature challengedness to easily get down from on his own!

Without further ado, or a word (let alone a warning), Robin grasped the Bear under the arms and whisked him effortlessly onto the floor.

He did this with such poise that the last of any aplomb that Reggie may have had left simply vanished – you could almost hear the noise it didn't really make!

As Reggie made his way from the Cabin into the Galley Robin called out "Do, please be very careful with the kettle, it will still be very hot."

Reggie turned around. He was obviously ready to deliver a cutting and almost certainly sarcastic, riposte.

But he didn't get the chance to deliver his reply however, as before he could actually respond, Robin went on "Don't be afraid to ask for help, it's always available and is, if you ask, always given freely and without judgement. There's no shame in admitting you need others from time to time."

There was another, almost audible, silent noise as the pomposity balloon that contained Reginald Arbuthnot Cholmondeley's prospective reply was 'popped'. Reggie knew, in his heart of hearts, that Robin was absolutely right and once again he revised his opinion of his Human for the better . . . . . .

CHAPTER 3 (continued)

Having successfully got down from the bed without waking his Human, Reggie momentarily interrupted his reverie and decided to make his way through the Boat towards the stern (that's the back to all you non-boat types!) as that was where he knew the broom was kept – and he had resolved that his tidying endeavours would involve sweeping.

As he wanted to make sure that Lettie didn't spoil the silence and wake Robin up, he very carefully and softly opened the Cabin door and slid through. Sure enough the Dog had instantly sussed that there was movement aboard so she had moseyed down from where she slept and was waiting outside the door to the Cabin. It came as no surprise to Reggie that her rear end was oscillating wildly! "Sorry girlie it's only me – no food or walkies yet". Using the 'W' word was not helpful however as it just made the Dog's tail's wagginess quotient increase several notches – up to eleven in fact!

Sliding the Cabin door closed again (all the doors on the Boat were that sort – it saved space apparently), Reggie resolved to make an attempt at seeing if he had got the Dog's confidence yet. "Come on Lettie, let's go aft". Much to his surprise (and delight!) Lettie actually followed him.

Being a Bear with a heightened degree of self-awareness did make Reggie wonder if she was only doing that because there was a possibility that the Bear had access to the food – but even with that *caveat* Reggie chalked up her obedience to his 'command' as a win!

By now Reggie knew his way around the Boat – frankly there wasn't *that* much of it - but he was a little uncomfortably aware that he didn't really *know* his way around yet! He didn't for example, know where Robin kept the chocolate biscuits – and Reggie was a Bear who liked to know where the chocolate biscuits were kept (just in case of chocolate biscuit deprivation emergencies of course, not because he was greedy or had a chocolate biscuit *problem*, you understand!)

54

"Oh Yes you do, you know!" Reginald Arbuthnot Cholmondeley recognised this voice (only audible in his own head) immediately as it was actually his own – it was the voice of his conscience! Anyone with any sort of standards (and the Bear had high ones!) occasionally hears from this, and Reggie heard his often enough to know better than to seriously argue with it.

"Well I wouldn't call it a problem, more a sporadic craving – which I totally have under control". Being the fundamentally honest Bear he was he knew that he wasn't even convincing himself. Luckily his conscience knew this and decided to let him get away with it – this time!

So, putting aside all or at least almost all thoughts of chocolate biscuits (well who doesn't have chocolate biscuits on their mind a lot of the time?) Reggie began a proper exploration of the place he was now quite happy to call 'Home' – and if he happened to come across the place where the chocolate biscuits lived then that would be simply serendipitous!

Immediately on leaving the Main Cabin (which as you already know, doubled as a study/den for Robin) and into the Saloon, he went past the door to the Head (which he had learnt was the strange 'boat' term for the bathroom).

Part of that room jutted into the Main Cabin – which is what made it such an interesting, non-square shape.

Robin had explained that he only used the Head onboard in emergencies (such as when it was raining). He much preferred to use the facilities in the shower block of the Marina in which AlexIan was moored, as he was entitled to do under the agreement for the mooring he had with the Marina owner. Having poked his nose inside the Head, Reggie understood one element of the reason for Robin's preference for using the amenities onshore – it was pretty cramped, even for the small(ish) Bear let alone the large Human!

The other reason was that eventually someone had to empty the loo – and, as Robin put it very succinctly, "Who else – me of course!" Reggie sympathised with Robin's wish to not have to undertake that particular chore more often than was necessary and also determined that he would try very hard not to give Robin any cause to blame him for having to do it earlier than was absolutely unavoidable!

Opposite the Head was the Guest Cabin where the Boys slept when they came for the whole weekend (generally Friday and Saturday nights – then they were usually taken back by Robin late Sunday afternoon).

Reggie hadn't really seen the inside of the Guest Cabin except during a brief tour of the Boat that Robin had given him so he took advantage of his chance to have a good look, slid the door open and looked inside.

It was, to coin a phrase, 'cosy but comfy'. In other words not very big, but inviting nonetheless – snug!

There was an especially clever bed arrangement – bunks (one practically on the deck and the other about 3 feet above it). Robin had told Reggie how this system was so clever. Apparently you could quite easily rearrange the bunk beds into one single double bed.

"Naturally" he explained, "in that configuration there isn't much room for anything other than getting in and out of the bed; but at least it means I can have couple type friends over and offer them accommodation if they want to stay – or if they have had a little too much to drink and *need* to stay because neither of them can drive!"

Reggie was impressed by this use of the limited available area; just like he was with most other aspects of the interior of the Boat that he had seen so far. He liked the design and utility of things and the extraordinarily ingenious use of the relatively small amount of space.

Because it was primarily for the Boys use it had quite a lot of their stuff in it – and it all was, bluntly but truthfully, a bit of a mess!

Reggie had already made an executive choice – namely that he wouldn't begin to start his tidying up in there. He had justified this by pointing out to himself that he wouldn't know where things went and he didn't Robin getting into trouble with the

Boys when they came down next and were unable to find a particular toy, book, item of clothing or anything else. Well, as an excuse (which is what it *really* was) it wasn't great (and wouldn't stand up to a lot of careful scrutiny) but it worked for him.

The real reason was that he wasn't confident enough in his neatening skills yet to think of what he would be able to do in the Boys Room as 'shipshaping' and he didn't want to do a second (or third or fourth) rate job because he wanted Robin to be pleased with him – and not to feel that he had to just *say* he was pleased while secretly being mildly disappointed.

Moving aft he came into the Saloon proper. On his left was the Galley – with the cooker, fridge and various cupboards (above and below) up against the side of the Boat. The rest of the space was taken up with comfy chairs towards the back ("I mean aft" he mentally corrected himself) and a dining table and chairs in the other corner.

As he looked down the Saloon, to his left was a little door, which Robin had told him went down into the hold – where there was a freezer and various storage boxes. It was also where the engine compartment was. So to stop curious small people getting in there the door was securely closed and locked with a very business-like padlock.

Just next to the little door were some steps leading up to the door to the Wheelhouse – which is exactly what it sounds like. Reggie made his way towards those steps and then climbed up them. In this instance 'climbed' is a very precise description – because they were just that little bit too high for Reggie to get up them easily. Fortunately for his rather exaggerated, sense of his own dignity there was nobody but Lettie to see him execute this graceless manoeuvre – and he was pretty sure she'd keep quiet about it!

During all Reggie's wanderings through the Boat the Dog had been pootling around – nosing into stuff on the floor, trying to get into the Boys' Room when Reggie had opened the door ("No, stay out," the Bear had ordered which, to Reggie's huge satisfaction, she obeyed). When Lettie saw that they were going into the Wheelhouse she was suddenly very interested – *this* was the way you went when 'walkies' were in prospect! Luckily for Reggie he was already on the top step and had a tight hold on the door handle when four legs, a body and an incredibly waggy tail joined him, otherwise there would have been an 'incident'!

As Reggie opened the sliding door Lettie pushed past him and made straight for the door to the land outside – which was firmly closed and locked with the brother of the padlock to the hold. She sat down (but still somehow managed to keep her tail wagging) and looked meaningfully at the Bear.

"Sorry girlie, not yet, you'll have to wait for Robin to wake up before you get to go out". She seemed to understand and with only the briefest look of disappointment and resignation, bounded back down the steps into the Saloon where she curled up on her blanket, heaved a sigh, and waited patiently for the next opportunity to present itself.

Reggie walked purposefully towards the starboard side of the Wheelhouse. In case you don't know 'Starboard' means the right hand side of the Boat (when facing forrard – the correct way of saying towards the prow, or front). There was another door to the outside here as well (also secured with a padlock) but this led to the side of the Boat where the water was – so was strictly out of bounds to all and sundry!

Next to the door however, was what Reggie had come for – a stiff bristled broom propped up against the wall. The broom seemed to be 'at rest' – but the Bear couldn't help thinking that it was standing there with an air of readiness just waiting to start sweeping.

"Don't be ridiculous." As there was no one about Reggie said this out loud. "It's just a broom after all." Much as he tried to persuade himself of this he found that he couldn't shake the feeling that there was a distinct element of 'alive' about the broom. He was of course right. There were still traces of the tree that it was made of and so some of the 'treeness' remained – albeit that it was now really only focused on it's primary task of sweeping. It's other job, which amounted essentially to just standing there and waiting, was easy as that is pretty much what it had done all the time it was still a tree.

Reginald Arbuthnot Cholmondeley gave himself a medium rated stern talking to ("Even if it has some degree of awareness it can't be cross with me for using it for the purpose for which it is designed, surely?"). This obviously worked for him as without a second thought (let alone a third or fourth), he marched across the Wheelhouse and grasped the broom firmly.

"Right, let's kick some dirt's bottom!"

Taking a firm grip on the broom's handle Reggie looked around the Wheelhouse.

As soon as he saw what a mess there was to 'kick the bottom of', he realised that he should have formulated a sweeping plan *before* taking hold of the broom.

In addition it didn't help that he hadn't quite appreciated just how tall (and heavy!) the ex-tree was compared to him. Put simply, the part of the broom he was holding was rather closer to the floor end than he would have liked – and there was a lot more broom extending above him than he was comfortable with.

It was too late to stop now even if there wasn't anyone except Lettie to point out his failure were he to do that – and he was confident that she wouldn't tell Robin that either. It certainly helped that she wasn't actually watching him (he had quickly checked). Still, the Bear was not the sort of Bear that started something and then gave up – notwithstanding that he could get out of it without anyone knowing. "But *I* will know though," was all he had to say to himself on that subject.

The die was cast.

There were two very important questions that needed deciding upon however – how much sweeping should he do and should he just deal with the Wheelhouse or the Saloon as well?

It was a genuine dilemma - but the Wheelhouse *really* was a mess and needed sorting out far more than the Saloon did.

Reggie had admired Robin's use of it as a sort of airlock, getting the Boys to take off all their grubby stuff – like gloves, wellie boots, jackets and for one of them at least, trousers!

"No names, no pack drill," said the Bear to himself – from somewhere in his head came a memory that made him aware that he knew what it was like to be classed as the 'messy' one and felt that even though he was the only one in his head, it was much fairer to keep the knowledge of which of the Boys warranted that particular nickname to himself.

"Anyhooo, this is not getting things done".

Reginald Arbuthnot Cholmondeley was only too conscious of the fact that he was prevaricating – and that was both simply unacceptable and not getting the task he had set himself done.

"Right! Sweep the Wheelhouse. Then if there's enough time, I'll have a go at tidying the Saloon."

Although he felt much better for having reached a resolution, the time had come to wield the broom – and he was by no means confident of his ability in that regard.

Reggie managed to postpone the inevitable for a few more seconds while he reconnoitred and made a plan (well that's what he told himself – but it was obvious he was just putting off using the broom, which was getting larger in his estimation with each second he wasted).

Finally he moved to one corner and began sweeping. As is so often the way with things one keeps avoiding, once he stopped fretting and started doing he appreciated how completely misplaced (not to say ridiculous!) all his fears had actually been.

"Well," he said to no one in particular, "what on earth was I worried about."

Using basic physics (the principles applying to levers) Reggie got into a rhythm quite quickly and before he knew it, he had accumulated quite a pile of dirt – and an enormous sense of satisfaction at a job well done.

Unfortunately when he stopped sweeping (just for a moment, not for a rest – honestly) and looked at the quantity he had collected he saw, with some clarity and a momentary feeling of panic, just how very much there actually was!

He gulped and then said to himself, "Okey dokey Mr Clever Clogs, so what do we do with this lot then?"

Luckily for him, this time Reggie managed to completely bypass flustered and went straight to rational thought.

He looked around the Wheelhouse and saw, as he had half expected to (and had wholly hoped to), a dustpan and brush (relatively much smaller than the broom – to the Bear's immense relief) propped up next to where the broom lived. These were also made of wood (except for the bristles of the brush). "OK," he thought, "that's the right tools – but what do I do with the actual dirt?"

With his newly acquired 'can do cleaning' attitude, the answer came with little effort – get the key for the padlock (he had seen where Robin had hidden it – to keep it safe from the Boys) and put it off the Boat. His logic was that as all the detritus had come from outside, it could legitimately go back there.

Unfortunately he didn't completely think this idea through let alone make a plan. You can probably guess what the problem was going to be.

He put the broom back where it lived and went down into the Saloon.

Lettie lifted her head inquisitively but on recognising there was no prospect of either food or walkies, put it back down with a mildly disenchanted snort.

Luckily the padlock key was not kept too high for Reggie to get at easily.

Reggie made a mental note, "I must remember to tell Robin to put the key somewhere else, maybe one of the upper cupboards, just in case the Boys decide to get it out and use it to escape!"

Of course he didn't mean that the Boys really wanted to 'escape' as such – but it showed a degree of consideration for their safety that he was prepared to get the key put out of his own reach simply so that the Boys wouldn't have the temptation of doing something which might cause them to be hurt, or for anything else to happen that could cause Robin to be worried sick.

Going back into the Wheelhouse he closed the door to the Saloon ("Mustn't let the Dog get off the Boat.") and walked to the port side to open the door.

The padlock was quite heavy and unwieldy, but he didn't let that stop him and soon the door to the outside was sliding back.
This turned out to be a big mistake as the wind whooshed in and blew the neat mound everywhere!
"*Rotten Raspberries*, I should have factored that in!"

Reggie's reaction was understandable in the circumstances – all his hard work had been undone in less time than it takes to eat a piece of chocolate!

Reggie slid the door closed, heaved a huge sigh and then went back over to get the broom to start his chore over again.

He had a bit of a brainwave. This time, when he had moved the dirt into a heap, he went into the Saloon and got two plastic bags from under the sink and put one inside the other. Taking the dustpan in one hand he tried to use the brush with the other, but he couldn't make that work as, smaller than the broom though it may have been, it was a bit big for his paws to enable him to operate successfully.

"Time for a bit of lateral thinking," he said. By now Reginald Arbuthnot Cholmondeley was completely and utterly determined not to be beaten.

He slid the door to the outside open just a little. Not enough to let the wind in – he checked that most carefully ("Once bitten, twice shy!") – and then wedged the dustpan in the gap. He put the open padlock through the clasp on the frame and the one on the door to keep it from sliding open and then he proceeded to brush stuff into the dustpan. To his utter delight the plan worked and he managed to get a lot of it in. He then transferred that to the plastic bags (one inside the other – in case just one wasn't strong enough and broke!) by putting the mouth of the bags over the edge of the dustpan and gently tipping the latter up so that the dirt flowed into the latter. Then he went back to the, by now much smaller mound and repeated the process. After three more goes he had a full plastic bag and the Boat had a much less grubby Wheelhouse deck.

"Thank you," he said to the broom, dustpan and brush as he replaced them in their proper places, "for a job well done."

Obviously, as he grasped immediately after saying this, it was merely half done – he still had to get rid of the material in the bag! "No problem, that's the easy bit." He may have thought that but he hadn't bargained for just how much a bag full of earth weighs – almost too much for a small Bear (the right word, just not the right word to use to Reggie's face!) to carry. Summoning up all his willpower and adding that to his physical strength (such as it was!) and his absolute refusal to contemplate even the possibility of failure Reggie heaved the bag over the doorsill

and onto the walkway that ran round the outside of the Boat.

Very carefully he moved (well struggled to move is a better way to describe it!) the bag towards the edge of the Boat – after all falling in the water would definitely put a damper on things in more ways than one!

The objective was to get the dirt filled bag to the bin onto the shore close by to the Boat.

As he got to the side of the Boat the Bear took stock. "Small(ish) Bear, very heavy bag full of dirt, relatively large gap between Boat and land."

This seemed to sum things up perfectly, but it hardly helped as it did absolutely nothing to instil even the smallest bit of confidence in his ability to actually carry out the task he had before him.

After consideration of all the options (of which there were really none), he eventually acknowledged his limitations, accepted that he simply couldn't get it across to the bin and just left it outside the door for Robin to deal with later – at least it was tidy!

Having carefully closed and padlocked the door to the outside, Reggie crossed the Wheelhouse, opened the door to the Saloon and clambered down the steps.

This time Lettie didn't even bother to raise her head – just her eyebrows, and those only as a form of acknowledgement of the Bear's presence.

She now knew that Reggie was not on her list of people who either provided food or took her for a walk. In fact that list currently consisted of just one person – Robin.

As Reggie turned round he looked up at the table in the opposite corner on which was the remains of last night's supper – well scone remnants and a mug, to which Robin and Reggie had treated themselves to after the Boys had been picked up.

It just goes to show how much his attempt at shipshaping (which Reggie did consider pretty successful on the whole) had tired him out that all he thought of at the sight of food was, "Well of course I *am* looking forward to breakfast – but it can wait."

So, feeling very pleased with himself the Bear trudged over to the sofa, clambered up onto it and plonked himself down sighing as he did so a sigh of great contentment, achievement and relief that he had finished.

He closed his eyes and almost at once lapsed into a drowsy slumber, the sort where though not really awake you aren't actually asleep either!

Reggie's half asleep, half awake type thoughts returned to the events of the previous day.

"Now, where had I got to?"

He thought for a moment and then, as it came to him, said "Oh, yes, now I remember."

The Bear's thought processes once again trailed off into contemplation.

. . . . . . When Reggie had got into the Galley he found that Robin had put the stepladder stool next to the sink – so as to allow the Bear to get up to it without help.

This small kindness didn't escape the Bear's attention. "Remember that Reggie." he thought, " It may be a little thing, but it really has made all the difference." As the hob was adjacent (with the kettle on it – "Remember it's still very hot, so be careful," Reggie reminded himself) he could pick it up and pour some of the recently boiled water into the sink, which he duly did. Opening the cold tap a little (*that* was a bit of a stretch but he made it on his own) he waited until he thought the water would be cool enough to put his paws in but warm enough to make washing worth it. He stopped the cold flow and then cautiously tested the temperature.

He was well chuffed to find that he had managed to time the exercise to perfection, as the water wasn't too hot nor was it too cold, it was *just right*!

Recognising that time was of the essence he quickly washed paws and face, cleaned his teeth, thoroughly rinsed the sink out and then dried himself off with the towel Robin had left out for him (a hand towel, big enough for a Bear's bath sheet) and made his way back into the Cabin.

Laid out on the armchair awaiting his return, were some of the purchases Robin had made for him on their way back from Barbara's house.

Obviously the Bear's 'smart clothes' were not appropriate for wearing on the Boat (plus they were nowhere near ready!), so it was determined (by Robin) that they would be kept for best and that Robin and Reggie would stop off at the little shop in the village where they sold children's clothes.

This suggestion had caused an incipient outburst of Bear pomposity but, before it escaped there was an assertive "Don't get huffy Reggie, they're the only things, apart from bespoke stuff, that will fit you!" from Robin (who was beginning to be familiar and able to deal, with some of the Bear's more regular moods).

This immediately stopped Reginald Arbuthnot Cholmondeley in his tracks – especially when he realised what an utter idiot he was in danger of being!

In fact, and much to the Bear's surprise and joy (both of which Robin noticed but chose not to comment on) the clothes in the shop were both of good quality and stylish – in his head Reggie believed himself to be a bit of a fashion icon and, as has already been demonstrated, he wasn't happy at having to put up with what he considered sloppy dressing.

They had left with loads of bags - shirts, tee shirts, trousers, jumpers, and sweatshirts – in fact a complete wardrobe!

All the way from the shop back to the Boat the Bear looked like he was purring with delight (simply the best word to describe his expression). He was still dressed in the tracksuit, and he couldn't wait to get changed into something from his new wardrobe.

Robin untied Lettie from the post outside the shop (where they had left her for safety) and off they went.

No prizes for guessing who was carrying all the bags. Hint: it wasn't the Bear and it certainly wasn't the Dog!

When they were a little outside the village Reginald Arbuthnot Cholmondeley made a sort of 'ahem!' noise and looked pointedly at the Dog.

"OK Reggie I'll ask her." Robin knew right away what Reggie was hinting at.

Lettie seemed totally cool with the whole 'Bear riding on my back' thing, so after Reggie got on again (in, it must be said, a rather more practised, but still not exactly elegant manner than before) off they went again.

The clothes Robin had chosen for Reggie to wear the day the Boys were coming consisted of a pair of comfy hard-wearing but tasteful, dark brown corduroy trousers, a plain white tee shirt and an equally plain green sweat shirt. Hanging up on the row of hooks next to the Wheelhouse door was a deep brown wax jacket with lots of pockets and a darker brown cord collar. This was Reggie's special favourite of all the things Robin had bought him. He also had a rather 'spiffy' flat cap.

Reggie could easily imagine how he'd look – very much the Country Bear (well his idea of how one of those looked anyway!).

Robin noticed the Bear looking at the neat pile on the chair. "C'mon Reggie," he said, "no time to waste, they'll be here soon."

Reggie was far too entranced at the thought of how he would look when dressed to notice the note of impatience and mild panic in Robin's voice – which is a good indicator of just how much he liked his new things!

"If you don't get dressed *tout suite* you'll be getting introduced in your nightshirt and I'm sure that doesn't sit well with your sense of propriety."

On being told in no uncertain terms, to "Get a move on!" (not *actually* said as such but it was certainly implied) Reginald Arbuthnot Cholmondeley snapped out of his contemplation of how good he was going to look and commenced getting on with actually getting to look good!

He was so engrossed in dressing that he forgot to be embarrassed at getting undressed in order to get dressed – probably because he had come to terms with there being little room for many of the niceties of personal privacy on the Boat.

In no time at all he was fully clothed, had folded his nightshirt and placed it (well 'stuffed' would be a better way of putting it – it was a bit high for him to be careful) under the pillow on the bed.

"Right, I'm ready." Instead of the congratulations he was expecting Robin just muttered "About time too," and carried on shipshaping.

Putting aside his natural urge to give voice to a barbed comment, Reggie swallowed hard and simply said, "So how can I help?"

There was, it should be said, a small element of acidity in his voice, but mostly he choked that aspect back because he acknowledged that it would be unfair of him to feel hard done by in all the circumstances and he could tell that Robin was feeling under pressure.

Reggie started thinking, "I can't imagine why he's stressed out, after all what's different about his Boys coming down to see him this time, surely he should be happy?" He only got as far as "why" however, before he had a minor epiphany – it was *his* presence that was so very, very different this time. He mentally 'gulped' and started to feel a little of the anxiety that, like an amorphous cloud of frayed nerves, pervaded the Boat.

"*Crush me a Cumquat*, I hope they like me."

As is often the way all these thoughts flashed through the Bear's head in no time at all, which was just as well as otherwise he might have missed Robin's reply to his enquiry about helping, and doing that would only have added to the Human's existing stress levels!

Robin pointed to the rest of Reggie's new clothes that had been decanted from the bags and were now in a neat pile on the armchair and said "Please put those away in the bottom two drawers of the tallboy in the Boys' room, and, no, that isn't a dig at your height ("Or lack of!" He only said that bit in his head), that is what that particular piece of furniture is called." Without waiting for a derisive snort, acerbic rejoinder or a *look* Robin carried on, "I have moved stuff out of them to give you room to keep your clothes tidy. You must have noticed that shipshape and Bristol fashion, which means neat and tidy in 'boat', is a basic requirement and if I, not generally known for my neatness, have to operate in accordance with an alien set of rules then so do you!" Reggie was by nature tidy (in his head anyway!) so this was not an issue with him.

"Aye aye Captain," said Reginald Arbuthnot Cholmondeley, who just couldn't resist snapping off a reasonable facsimile of a naval salute as he did so.

Robin barely noticed the sarcasm as he was on his way aft to sort out more stuff that needing organising.

Reggie left him to it and got on with his own task of putting his clothes away. He finished doing that in next to no time.

"I've finished Robin is there anything else I can do to help?"

Robin's reply was inaudible so Reggie walked through to the Saloon to ask that Robin repeat himself.

Much to the Bear's surprise and consternation, Robin was nowhere to be seen – either in the Saloon or in the Wheelhouse (at least the bit of it visible through the open door).

Reggie made his way aft. As he was negotiating the steps to the Wheelhouse (not something he was able to do without looking slightly silly!) he heard voices outside. He also noted a distinct lack of Dog on the Boat!

With a flash of inspiration (and a little bit of dread) Reginald Arbuthnot Cholmondeley came to the inescapable conclusion. "Gosh! The Boys must have arrived!"

Momentarily panic stricken Reggie thrashed around in his head for the best place to be waiting for the Boys. After all you only get one chance to make a first impression and he so very much wanted this one to be memorable – in a good way!

With a faint, but still nonetheless abnormal, note of regret in his voice he muttered, "Why couldn't I be a little less narcissistic? Instead of preening myself over how good I look (even though I certainly do! No you fool stop that at once, make the effort, get with the programme!) I should have been concentrating on the important issue – making sure Robin's Boys think well of me from moment one!"

There was no time to lose, and even less to make a decision but luckily, centuries of breeding in decisiveness came to his rescue (at least that was to what, when he thought about it later, he accredited his ability to reach a decision so swiftly).

"Of course, I know, sitting on the sofa in the Saloon apparently nonchalant ready to get up and be introduced."

Now while this may not seem a matter of great significance to everybody, it unquestionably was to Reginald Arbuthnot Cholmondeley who was, in case it hasn't been mentioned before, a very well brought up Bear with high standards of behaviour and ethics, as well as a highly developed moral code, for whom good manners were an essential part of one's character.

In next to no time the Bear somehow got back down the steps between the Wheelhouse and Saloon (best to draw a veil over exactly how he got down – frankly it wasn't pretty, and it certainly wasn't graceful!), made his way across the Saloon, reached the sofa, scrambled up with little or no thought for the elegance of the manoeuvre and ensconced himself on it (repeating the comment about the steps here should be unnecessary – but it is just as apt, only this time it is about 'up' and not 'down'!).

He also managed (and even he has no idea how he was able to do this!) to arrange his torso, head and various limbs in what, he hoped, appeared to be a nonchalant position and what's more, one that looked like it had been established for some time.

"Right," he said to no one in particular (there was nobody there to say it to anyway!), "I'm ready – bring them on!"

Luckily (for it was almost entirely due to the intervention of Lady Luck that he was actually ready) it was just in time – because as soon as he was in place he heard the sound of two sets of feet jumping onto the Boat, followed immediately by the four paws of the Dog.

Robin's Boys had arrived! "Showtime!" said Reggie to himself. The Bear swallowed hard once more and by sheer force of willpower, pushed trepidation to the back of his mind and nervousness out of his head. He really was ready for anything – or so he thought! . . . . . .

Reginald Arbuthnot Cholmondeley woke up with the sort of start that makes your whole body jerk with a little, but very noticeable spasm.

This was quite decidedly 'Not A Good Thing' as it caused a particularly unpleasant jarring of the rather irritating crick in his neck that as a result he instantly noticed he had.

As a way to try to ignore the pain he tried to work out how he had got it – and he deduced that it had been caused by his posture where he had been sleeping awkwardly on the sofa.

It was though quite clear what had woken him – the alarm had gone off!

Fortunately Robin had remembered to set it to radio again so it was much gentler than the last time that that particular device had instigated a state of general wakefulness on the Boat!

"Reggie, where are you?"

It was clear that Robin was also awake and had evidently noticed the lack of Bear in his vicinity!

"I'm in the Saloon Robin," Reggie replied, "I woke up early and thought I'd do a bit of shipshaping before you came to."

Reggie knew that it was only tidying and probably not worthy of the term 'shipshaping', but he thought he'd run it up the flagpole and see if Robin saluted it!

Robin came into the Saloon, still in his night things, took a quick look around the room and then, rather pointedly made no comment at all on the efficacy of the alleged shipshaping – but his face expressed a certain disappointment at the state of things.

Before the look on the Human's face (which Reggie saw and instantly understood) could translate into words the Bear quickly interjected, "No, not in here – in the Wheelhouse."

Reggie could instantly tell that Robin immediately regretted the unworthy and as it turned out, incorrect notion that had been going through his head and he decided to forgive him, just this once mind, as Robin had after all only woken up a few minutes before and was visibly not firing on all cylinders yet.

Taking the few steps necessary (for him) to reach the other end of the Saloon, Robin peered through the window in the door to the Wheelhouse.

As he turned round Reggie knew that all his hard work of earlier had been to good effect, as Robin had a huge grin on his face.

"Wow Reggie, great job, you'd hardly know that the small persons had been anywhere near there."

Puffing himself up with pride (which his aching neck told him was a mistake) Reginald Arbuthnot Cholmondeley contented himself with a simple "It was nothing." It had been something of course, but modesty at this point seemed the best option.

"How on earth did you manage it, that broom is really heavy?" Robin asked.

"Application of simple physics principles, and a bit of ingenuity." False modesty, he thought, is all very well, but now when asked a straight question to which the only straight answer is one which makes you look good!

Reggie went on, "I am afraid that I had to leave the bag of dirt just outside the Wheelhouse door though. It was my intention to take it to the bin but I'm sorry to say that I simply couldn't move it any further."

As he said this, Reggie realised that he was actually more annoyed at himself because of the fact that he had been unable to finish the task he had set himself than he was proud of what he had achieved.

Robin, on the other hand, was both impressed and pleased not to say rather surprised; with the apology (which he felt was totally unnecessary) and the uncharacteristic display of humility – the lack of which was frankly, normally one of Reginald Arbuthnot Cholmondeley's least endearing traits!

Storing the possible ramifications of this apparent change in Reggie's attitude for later consideration (it went in the 'Note to Self' section of his brain), Robin did his best to bolster and pump back up what to him seemed to be a slight deflation of Reginald Arbuthnot Cholmondeley's ego!

"Absolutely *pas de probleme* Reggie. I'm very impressed and very grateful."

This had the desired (and intended) effect in that it made Reginald Arbuthnot Cholmondeley's ego sit up and take notice again.

Robin went on, "Sweeping out the Wheelhouse was the one job I knew I would have to do before I go off to work because otherwise all the dirt in there could very easily have made it way into everywhere else so not having to do it is just great. Thanks again Reggie."

It seemed that once more, Lady Luck was batting for Reggie that morning, given that he had only done the Wheelhouse chore because he couldn't face doing the Saloon tidying. Result! "OK then," said the Bear's conscience, " because you did work really hard we'll keep *that* truth from Robin."

"No argument from me on that." Reggie replied to himself (as his conscience is, naturally, just a part of himself). Another result!

Robin went back into the Cabin to get his washing stuff.

When he came back out about two minutes later, dressed in his 'floppies' (essentially comfy elasticated tracksuit trousers and a sweatshirt) he asked "Are you coming over to the shower block with me?" His face took on a rather puzzled look as he went on, with a small, but marked, degree of wariness in his voice, "Sorry Reggie, but I don't actually know if you have showers or such like – after all you are furry everywhere and as we found out yesterday getting you dry once you are wet all over is a bit of a business – especially with no hairdryer!" This was undoubtedly true as the Bear remembered only too well (albeit with a wry smile from remembering all the fun they had had before he got wet!) from the day before, but he was unsure whether to take umbrage at what was clearly a rather personal enquiry into his ablutionary habits. He decided that it was a perfectly reasonable question so he said by way of explanation, "I am really very lucky in that I don't need to wash all over that often – my fur has certain enzymes and the like which repel dirt. Obviously I need to clean my face and paws regularly but full on showers, no, they

77

are not necessary on a frequent basis. I will however, happily accompany you over there if you would like."

Robin smiled and said, "That would be most acceptable."

Reggie nipped into the Cabin to put 'his' tracksuit on. All the sartorial horrors he had felt and agonies he had gone through at wearing such an ill-fitting garment (which hardly sat well or at all with his own view of himself as a fashionable Bear about Town) had now gone the way of certain other preconceived ideas he had previously held about what was and what, more importantly, most definitely was thoroughly *not* tolerable as clothing or indeed, certain behavioural traits.

Being on the Boat, and being exposed to Robin (and the Boys!) was toning down his innate snobbery and pretentiousness about a fair few number of things – and he was contentedly aware that he felt all the happier for it.

While all this had been going on Lettie had been bouncing all

around the Boat – rushing between the Saloon and the Cabin, generally getting in the way and being, technically at least, a real nuisance (but neither Robin or Reggie minded as they knew she was excited and made allowance for this).

Of course Lettie knew *exactly* what this sort of activity meant at this time in the morning – 'walkies' followed by food, just about her two favourite things.

When the Bear came back the Dog made a beeline (well, more a 'dogline') for the door to the Wheelhouse, standing with her front paws on the top step and her tail wagging at about twenty-seven to the dozen!

"OK girlie, let me get the door open." As Robin said this he started sliding the door back and the Dog squeezed herself through ("How *does* she do that?" thought Reggie) and then rushed over to the door to the outside, where she did the 'front paws, tail' thing again; this time with occasional glances back at Robin as if to say, "Come on, come on, get it open, let's go, what's the hold up, when are we going?" Reggie got exhausted just watching her!

Eventually (it was quite quickly actually, but in Dog terms it was practically forever!) Robin undid the padlock and slid the outer door back. Once again the Dog did her squeezing act. When she had made it out of the door, she then leapt without effort but still wagging her tail, over the water where she began chasing round and

round. This was clearly her way of expressing impatience at how long it was taking Robin and Reggie to join her.

Reggie was, as he had been on the other occasions he had seen Lettie when she had been let off the Boat, very impressed with the fact that she didn't simply rush off madly in an 'away' sort of direction but waited patiently (well patiently for a dog!) until given permission to go – at which point she went.

He commented on this by saying to Robin, "Isn't Lettie well behaved?"

Robin was in fact rightly very proud of Lettie. She was, he felt, very well behaved – especially when compared to many other dogs who in his view unquestionably were not! That isn't to say, of course, that Lettie wasn't completely potty (she was) or that she didn't run off when given her head and permission to do so (she did that – but always came back when called).

"No such thing as a bad dog Reggie, just bad owners!" Robin pontificated, "Lettie knows when she can go crazy and when it's time to be sensible, we've had lots and lots of long talks about the difference and I know she gets it."

People who didn't keep their dogs under control or who mistreated them were two of Robin's 'pet hates', as he had made quite clear yesterday when they were out with the Boys!

Robin stepped off the Boat and onto the land, then offered his hand to make it easier for the Bear to get across the gap. Reggie quite cheerfully accepted his assistance and off they went across the Marina to the showers with Lettie alternately bounding away and then back to them – she knew that this was allowed at this point in the morning routine.

When they got to the shower block Robin asked Reggie if he wanted to wash there or wait until they got back to the Boat. "On the Boat please, if it's all the same to you," said the Bear, who was enjoying the crisp morning air.

"No probs. Lettie you do as Reggie tells you, OK?" The Bear was certain he saw the Dog nod!

While waiting for Robin to complete his *toilette* the Bear thought some more about what had happened the day before.

. . . . . . So there was Reggie, having just managed, by the skin of his teeth, to get himself ensconced on the sofa in the Saloon, looking as nonchalant as it was possible for him to look in the circumstances, because quite honestly, he was really quite nervous and that was an unaccustomed emotion for him!

If he had thought he was ready for anything (and he had thought that of course) he was sadly mistaken.

Jumping down, one after the other, into the Saloon, came what Reggie thought at first glance, were two smaller versions of Robin.

They weren't actually *that* small for people of their ages – one was only a little bigger than Reggie and the other was a little bit more bigger than that!

In reality (as the Bear came to notice as he got to know them better) they were indeed, a bit like their Father; but they were also a bit like their Mother (that was a guess on Reggie's part as he hadn't met or seen her, but it was right as it turned out!).

Mostly though they were without doubt very much their *own* people, both in looks and personality; although Reggie noticed quite a few of Robin's attitudes and character traits in them (mostly the good ones, but also some of the irritating ones!). As the day went on it became clear that there were quite a few phrases, mannerisms, attitudes and postures they used that *definitely* had 'My Daddy says/thinks/does this (or that)' written all over them!

Before Reginald Arbuthnot Cholmondeley had a chance to get up to introduce himself – or to *say* anything - they rushed past him and into the Guest Cabin. There were two 'thump' noises (caused by the two of them chucking their respective backpacks onto their respective beds) and then they burst back into the Saloon.

"Hi," they said in stereo, " you must be Reginald Arbuthnot Cholmondeley,"

The Bear's gast was well and truly flabbered and what little self-assurance he had managed to retain simply vanished!

On top of everything they had spelt his name right as well!

He didn't say anything for a moment but then, as he recovered his poise (admirably as he thought – but let's draw a veil over whether that's true or not!) sufficiently to reply, he said, "Yes, you are quite correct, indeed I am."

He paused momentarily, while he worked out which of them he reckoned was which, "and you must be Alex and Ian."

As he said this he looked at each one that he thought was the one whose name he'd said. "I am very pleased to meet you both," and he extended his right paw in their general direction, hoping that at least one of them would take and shake it!

Both the Boys tittered. Then the one who was a little bit more bigger than the Bear (who Reggie had decided, correctly as it happened, was Alex, the older one) managed to stop doing that, took hold of the proffered paw, shook it and said, "How do you do My Lord. I am Alexander and this is my brother Ian."

As he said this he used his left hand to gesture at his brother, who visibly composed himself a bit and said, while still, however, grinning hugely, "Hello there."

Alex turned to face him and whispered, "You forgot to say 'My Lord' doofus."

Having had his error pointed out to him Ian said, "Oh dear, terribly sorry My Lord."

Reginald Arbuthnot Cholmondeley was taken aback by the Boys' display of good manners, but he controlled his flabbergastedness (although he still hadn't got rid of it altogether) enough to say, "Oh my goodness let's not stand on ceremony. Please do call me Reggie."

The situation finally got the better of the Bear and he burst into almost uncontrollable fits of laughter – to be joined pretty much simultaneously, by Robin and both of the Boys.

In between the guffaws and trying to breathe Reggie found space and time to think to himself, "Phew, well that seems to have gone all right then!"

That really was typical English massive understatement. It hadn't just gone 'all right' – it was just about the best start ever! . . . . . .

The last bit of CHAPTER 3

Reggie stood outside the shower block and looked all around at the Marina. Every now and then he would call out, "Come here, Lettie," when he felt she was wandering off a little bit too far away. In fact he was wrong about the distance thing but Lettie came back anyway – Robin had told her that the Bear had been left in charge and anyway, she realised that he wasn't quite as sensible in dog terms, as Robin was – at least not just yet!

There were boats up on blocks in varying stages of completeness (they were being cleaned up and serviced for going back in the water – and that entailed bits being taken off, dealt with and then put back on) and all sorts of 'boatie' stuff – anchor balls and chains, masts, cables (large ropes), fenders and lots and lots of other things that Reggie simply didn't recognise or couldn't put a name to. He could see lots of vessels, with plenty of different shapes and sizes, tied up alongside by ropes snaking from forrard, stern and, if necessary due to the length of the craft, amidships (that's the middle of a boat – as I am sure you guessed) onto bollards on the shore.

Reggie could see Alexlan way off in the distance, right at the edge of the Marina, which gave him a warm 'there's home' feeling.

Eventually Robin came out still rubbing his head with his big towel. "Right, that's me all clean and sparkly and undoubtedly more awake than I was. Let's go Reggie. Lettie, come here girlie."

The last bit was obviously directed to the Dog who pricked up her floppy ears and because she recognised the voice and command, started trotting back on a course set to intercept Robin and Reggie about 30 yards along an imaginary line from the shower block to the Boat.

Reggie noticed this and once again impressed at the Dog and her instinctive use of angles, said, "Look at that Robin – isn't Lettie clever."

"She certainly is, in her own very doggie sort of way." Robin replied, "But I still haven't been able to teach her to cook, let alone wash up!" He laughed out loud at this piece of obvious nonsense, and Reggie joined in!

All three of them made their way back to the Boat in a very jolly frame of mind – notwithstanding that the morning was, understating it rather, more than a bit nippy!

When they got back on board Robin started to get Lettie's food ready. This was met unsurprisingly, by a display of manic wagginess from the Dog. Indeed there was so much 'waggy' that Reggie was nearly blown over as he walked round behind her!

"I'm sure that I could do that in future Robin," the Bear said, "If you would like me to?" As he was saying this he was thinking, "How difficult can it be to open a can and put food from it into a bowl?"

"That would be great if you would Reggie, ta everso."

Robin pointed to a cupboard and said, "The tins of food are under there. She gets half a tin per meal." Then he pointed to a drawer, "The can opener is in here, as are the plastic lids for the part used tins, and the dog food forks are kept in the divider next to it. They are clearly marked 'Dog Food Only', just in case."

Then he said, "Not that there is anything inherently wrong with Lettie's food you understand, but I don't really want to eat my food with anything that has been anywhere near hers thank you very much!"

This made perfect sense to Reggie who made a careful note of where the canine cutlery was kept.

Having sorted out Lettie, Robin went into the Cabin saying as he did so, "Right, time to get dressed for work, back in a mo' guys and gals."

While Robin was getting ready for work Reggie ambled over to the sofa and climbing up onto it (he was getting better at doing that and had actually stopped being embarrassed when other people saw him!), picked up his book and began reading.

"OK, time for me to go then. Will you be alright here on your own?" Robin had come back in next to no time and had caught Reggie on the hop a bit.

"I shall be fine and I won't be on my own will I? Lettie and I will keep each other company," the Dog went all waggy again at the mention of her name although Reggie took that to be a sign of assent.

"Cool beans. If you feel up to taking her for a short w-a-l-k," (Robin spelt it out as the actual word had a dramatic and occasionally disastrous effect on Lettie – even when she had only just had one!), "then you have the plank across the gap betwixt the Boat and the shore now. Up to you of course but I recommend not going too far, and please definitely *not* outside the confines of the boatyard." This made perfect sense to Reggie, who frankly was not entirely sure he was up to leaving the Boat on his own yet – let alone with Lettie – so he nodded and said, "Understood."

Robin then looked sternly(ish) at the Dog, on whom the look had no effect – she just sat there happily wagging her entire rear end and making little happy doggie noises. The reality is that it wouldn't have made any difference even if Robin had been able to carry off actually adopting an uncompromising expression and tone of voice, which he didn't and couldn't – it's very difficult to do when you have such a floppy, waggy canine looking at you with such a trusting and generally devoted face.

"Right," he said, completely giving up on the whole 'stern' thing, "Reggie is in charge girlie, *capice*?"

Not for the first time Reggie could have sworn that Lettie not only understood but also quite deliberately nodded in acknowledgement of her instructions.

Robin turned back to Reggie, "I can't get back at lunchtime today, so even if you just let her off the Boat on her own for a bit that would be helpful." He stopped, had a thought, and then added somewhat dubiously, "Obviously keep an alert eye on her though."

Reggie instantly understood that he was being trusted with an enormous responsibility and he mentally gulped!

Robin picked up his bag and with a cheery "Have a good day, see you both later," left the Bear and Dog to their own devices.

Lettie, for whom this was the norm, pootled over to her blanket in the Saloon and settled down for a good paw and face cleaning session.

Reggie was, momentarily, unsure of what to do next, so he pulled himself up onto the sofa again and began to ponder. Almost without thinking his mind wandered back to the day before.

The last bit of CHAPTER 3 ½

. . . . . . After they had done the whole introduction bit the Boys plonked themselves down on the sofa, one either side of Reggie. Without any discernible pause they just started chattering with the Bear about all sorts of stuff as if the three of them had known each other for ages – and Reggie, almost as if their enthusiasm was infectious, did so as well, also without any perceptible gap for thought. Robin looked at *his* Boys and *his* Bear (he knew what Reggie said about Bears having Humans etc., but today he felt as if it was the other way round) with an extremely satisfied look on his face – truth be told he was also mightily relieved at the way things had gone so far!

"I'm for a cup of tea, anybody want anything while I'm up?" He was, as he guessed he would be, instantly bombarded with demands from all three!

Having satisfied the requirements of Boys and Bear, albeit only temporarily as he well knew from past experience, Robin sat down on the armchair with his, already well earned, cuppa and considered trying to interrupt the gabblefest that was in full swing on his sofa. Boys and Bear had barely drawn breath to take the drinks and biscuits from the tray Robin presented them. His response to the Boys' actual victuals requests was a slightly curt, "No, it's too early for crisps and sausage rolls – I already get grief about the junk you eat when you're here, any worse and you'll get me shot!"

All of them however, had said "Thank you" – adding either "Robin" (from Reggie) or "Daddy" (the Boys) – which Robin counted as a result!

Robin's stress levels, which had been right off the scale, had dropped back to normal – well as normal as they ever were when his children were around!

Accordingly he decided that, as they were currently well involved with getting to know Reggie, he would relax (see his comments on 'normal'!), go with the flow, and enjoy his tea and, yes why not, a biscuit or two.

After two (OK four, but who's counting – no, really, who *is* counting!) shortbread biscuits Robin's 'Daddydar' picked up what he instantly knew to be an incipient conspiracy brewing in the general area of the sofa – the Boys and the Bear were plotting something!

"Right," he thought, "time to step in and take charge." Robin had a theory that if he thought positively enough then he just might be able to retain sufficient control over the Boys to make it at least appear that he was *actually* in control. Frankly the addition of Reggie to the mix, a loose cannon if ever there was one, made this idea less easy to put into practice – although the jury was still out onto which side the Bear would come down. Robin's best guess was that Reggie would take each situation as it came, and make a decision there and then, rather than being on any particular side. Not great, but he could live with that as it pretty much coincided with the way he had to live anyway. He wasn't sure what he would do if Reggie sided with the Boys – but that was a bridge to cross if (or when – aargh!) he came to it.

This makes it sound like parenting is a war – but it's a lot closer to that than those without direct, and personal familiarity with child interaction believe. In fact all good parents are just trying to keep their children safe and happy – with, as they all fervently hope, as little of either accidental blood and injury or embarrassment and general mayhem as possible!

Robin reckoned that with his newly acquired 'non-grownupness' he might have discovered an edge – but one as yet untested, so back up went his stress levels! This was entirely standard though, so he could deal with it.

Robin was only too well aware that being a Daddy is a 24/365 (366 in a Leap Year) occupation without holidays or parole – and he was cool with that. He also knew that, as a result of being a Daddy, he couldn't ever really truly relax – but he was cool with that too. Nevertheless, and let's make it clear right here and now (if it hasn't been made obvious so far), he completely, totally and absotively *loved* his Boys and *loved* being their Daddy. In point of fact Robin reckoned that it was his total immersion in the whole

'Daddy' concept and more importantly, the way in which he and his Boys interacted that had ungrown up him enough for Reggie to have picked him out as not only available *for*, but essentially sorely in need *of*, a Bear to look after him.

Dealing with offspring conspiracies was Parenting 101 – a basic skill that you just had to have. There were two ways to go. The first was to find out what they were plotting and make a decision on whether you approved (in which case let them get on with it) or, if you didn't, come up with something to distract and divert them from the intended course. The second way (which Robin went with this time – primarily because of the 'Reggie' incongruity) was simply to nip the whole thing in the bud by a pre-emptive strike!

"Anyone up for a walk with Lettie then?" This, Robin considered, was nothing short of genius – playing the Dog card! Lettie had, up to this point, just been sitting relatively quietly (for her) in front of the sofa patiently (for her). At the magic word 'walk' she instantly sprung into action – bounding about, putting her feet up on the sofa, licking any face she could get at (horrified splutters from Reggie at this!) and generally making herself attractive to the Boys as the centre of attention. Well, have you ever tried ignoring a dog that wants to go 'walkies' – it isn't the easiest thing on the world! Both the Boys were immediately diverted from whatever plans they had been hatching.

Conspiracy quashed therefore, and as Robin well knew, no conspiracy ever comes back from a proper quashing – which this categorically was. Result!

"Right then, the choices are round the harbour or off in the car somewhere, Southsea maybe, or perhaps a bit more country." Then Robin delivered the *coup de grace*, "And as you're only here for the day, I thought we'd get a pub lunch – how does that sound?"

All leftover thoughts of whatever anarchy they had been conniving at simply vanished as "Yes please," (Alex) and "Cool beans," (Ian) came from the Boys. Reggie chipped in with "All of that sounds splendid, thank you."

"Thank goodness winter's over and the weather's good enough to go out for some of the day," thought Robin, for whom entertaining the Boys inside when it was miserable, blowing a gale and wet was the definition of 'ghastly'.

After a short debate that honoured Robert's Rules of Order more in the avoidance than the observance, and which only ended when Robin had had more than enough and made a unilateral decision - "Right, a walk around the harbour; get down Lettie, all in good time; back here to change, then up to the Black Dog for lunch." Having made the choice Robin issued instructions. "Alex, Ian, wellies and coats, scarves, gloves and hats. Reggie do you need boots or can you cope with drying and brushing off your feet in the Wheelhouse?"

Reggie looked puzzled. "I do not allow grubby footwear into the Saloon. So, boots or not?" Taken aback by Robin's verbal onslaught, Reggie replied almost automatically, "Boots, if you have some my size please."

Robin was inwardly exultant and amused at the total lack of argument from Reggie, who had been caught well and truly on the back foot. "Certainly." He said, " No problem."

Robin turned to his younger son and said, "Ian, be a darling and go and root out your old boots from the cupboard please, they should fit Reggie."

Ian said, "Yes Daddy," and wandered off to find his old boots for the Bear.

"Alex poppet, can you please lend Reggie a scarf and a pair of gloves?"

"Of course I can Daddy. Come on Reggie, let's go and chose a scarf and find you some gloves that fit." And with this Alex took the unresisting Bear's hand and led him off to the Guest Cabin to search for accessories.

Reggie was all a dither; one moment he was helping the Boys refine their plan ("Goodness what *were* we going to do?" He just couldn't remember), and the next everything had changed. Robin had sold all three of them an exquisite dummy and now they were all dancing to the puppet master's tune! Then he appreciated what an utter idiot he was being. Robin was just exhibiting normal parenting skills and he, Reginald Arbuthnot Cholmondeley, 9th Viscount of the Salop Oak, had been well and truly suckered in!

While everyone else was occupied Robin nipped into the Cabin and quickly changed – he was so quick (or were the others just very slow?) that he got back into the Saloon before anyone else did.

Finally Reggie and the Boys came back, dressed for the prospective walk.

Reggie was wearing an old pair of Ian's wellies – plus a jolly scarf of Alex's and his own 'spiffy' cap – and he really *did* look 'spiffy' in it.

"Right, all ready?" Nods all round, "OK then, Let's go."

So off they went.

Robin's words had the same effect as if he had fired a starting pistol. The Boys and the Dog were so excited that they all rushed up the Wheelhouse steps (Lettie took them in a single bound) and over to the outer door – which was of course, still padlocked shut! When they got to it there was the usual scrimmage to get to be first out of the door, even though they all must have known (if they had only calmed down sufficiently to allow rational thought) that no one was

going anywhere until someone (namely Robin) removed the security device.

The fracas was punctuated by Robin's attempts to maintain some form of order ("No one gets out until I can get there to unlock the door," or "If you don't let me though we're none of us going anywhere," and the classic, "I can wait all day you know."). Eventually however, the padlock was off, the door slid back and Boys and Dog were on the shore.

For the record Lettie was first as she did her normal squeezing trick!

Having very sensibly opted to stand back a little from the melee, Reggie was perfectly placed to view all this and he was amazed, but also relieved, that nobody ended up in the water!

"After you Reggie," said Robin, who had to see to the business of closing and then locking the door by putting the padlock on the outside.

Once again Reginald Arbuthnot Cholmondeley found himself presented with the problem of getting from Boat to land. He was still working up to jumping when Robin finished securing the vessel and resolved the dilemma by the simple expedient of lifting Reggie up and taking the Bear across with him.

Startled, albeit grateful for the help, Reggie could only manage to articulate (and that's probably not the right word!) various incoherent splutterings.

Robin chose, rightly, to believe that somewhere in there were the words "Thank you."

If it hasn't been before, it should perhaps be made clear now that getting to *actual* land involved first stepping onto the long jetty, alongside which the Boat was moored. This was itself over the water, and one had to walk the length of it to get to *terra firma*. It was secured in place by big wooden posts driven into the mud. The key word here is 'mud – which meant that it didn't stay entirely still when one was on it!

Robin explained that the Boys really enjoyed doing the walk in the area to which they were going – primarily because of the fact that there were no roads to negotiate; and they knew that this meant that they were allowed considerably more leeway then they would otherwise have been.

Almost as if they had been asked to prove that this were the case, the Boys had run off towards the seawall and were already a good hundred yards away. Lettie had gone with them, plainly in an even more bouncy and waggy mood than normal. Then suddenly she stopped, turned round, looked at Reggie and Robin and raced back to them.

When she reached them she indulged in more bouncing, wagging and general doggie lunacy. Then she stopped dramatically again, turned round, looked towards the Boys and chased off back to where they were.

Reggie looked up at Robin and asked, "Is Lettie completely potty or what?"

Robin laughed, then replied, "Poor thing, she just doesn't have a clue as to whether she's coming, going or has had her brain turned to marshmallow! This always happens when we all go out and the Boys separate from me. She is after all part sheep dog so she does have the herding gene thing going on. Basically she knows she's supposed to be looking after Alex and Ian, but she is also, occasionally, drawn back to the one who is, nominally at least, her master – namely me!"

At that last bit he smiled ruefully, then went on, "The result is what you've just seen – back and forth and back and forth and so on *ad nauseam*. Luckily she never gets sick of doing it just confused poor thing and we all get tired out and want to go back long before she ever does. Frankly she wears me out!" Another laugh accompanied this, so it was obvious that the last bit was not really meant to be taken literally.

Meanwhile the Boys, who clearly knew the relevant protocols for this walk, had stopped where the seawall turned to go out of sight of where Robin and Reggie were. Lettie also recognised this spot and was trotting, less frantically than before (although that is relative – she was still particularly bouncy and waggy), back towards them occasionally stopping to look back at the Boys just to check they hadn't disappeared.

Robin waved in a general 'on you go then' sort of way and the Boys did just that – they went on. "Watch this," said Robin, somewhat gleefully. When Lettie (who was still on the way to Robin and Reggie) next turned to check on her charges – they had gone!

Unsurprisingly this created an error message in Lettie's head. She circled round, looked despairingly at Robin and having got the same wave from him that he had given the Boys, 'whooshed' off to where she had last seen Alex and Ian. She was very quick when she was in full flight so it took her no time at all to get there – and to see that far from vanishing as she had feared, the Boys were just round the corner and perfectly safe!

"I know it's mean to do that – but sometimes I just can't resist it, cos it *is* funny."

"Naughty Robin," thought Reggie – but he did inwardly giggle as poor Lettie's face had been an absolute picture!

"I don't think it would be a very good idea for you to even consider riding Lettie in the mood she's in," Robin said. "Would on my shoulders be OK?"

Reginald Arbuthnot Cholmondeley considered this. On the one hand he hated admitting to any weakness, on the other hand Robin already knew he wasn't very fit *and* only had little legs *and* got puffed out easily *and* was quite happy to ride on Lettie (which surely had to be less dignified than being on Robin's shoulders!) so actually the offer was both tactful and, let's be honest here Reggie, particularly welcome.

"Thank you very much Robin." he replied, "That would be most acceptable." There are times when dignity comes a very poor second to practicality, as he had come to understand and, albeit reluctantly, acknowledge.

In one obviously well practised movement Robin lifted Reggie up and swung the Bear onto his shoulders, saying as he did so, "Upsadaisy, Allez oop!" As these were the sorts of things that one said to small children in such circumstances, not to Noble Bears, clearly Robin had no intention of letting Reggie off the indignity hook entirely.

Once again however, pragmatism was uppermost in Reginald Arbuthnot Cholmondeley's thoughts, so he let it go and in all honesty, he rather enjoyed being swung up; and he was certainly grateful not to have to walk!

One other thing that Reggie noticed as soon as he was settled and comfy was the view – he was much higher above the ground than he normally was and got a completely different perspective on things.

"This is very cool Robin, thank you, I can see for miles from up here."

"Don't mention it Reggie, glad to be of assistance. You're hardly heavy you know." This was taken as a compliment – although Robin hadn't necessarily meant it as such!

"So, what am I looking at then?" said Reggie pointing right (which, because they were heading southwards was in the general direction of West).

"Well," said Robin, as he marshalled his thoughts and looked at

 the map in his head, "we are on the west side of Thorney Island. The water is part of Chichester Harbour, which is horseshoe shaped, bent around the bit we're on at the mo'." He stopped to think, then, after a second, said, "Technically the bit we are currently on isn't an island here, it becomes that a little further south." Realising that he was in imminent danger of diving head first into full blown 'way too much information, lecturing mode' he pushed a lot of what he *was* going to say back into the files in his brain he had taken it

from and went on, "OK, right over there is Portsmouth Harbour, then Portsea Island, which is what Portsmouth is on, then Langstone Harbour, then Hayling Island, which is the bit of land you can see over there;" he pointed across the water as he said this, "then Thorney; then, over the other side, the rest of Chi Harbour, and finally Bosham and the Witterings, with the Chichester Channel leading up to, and no surprise here, Chichester – which has a lovely cathedral."

"Gosh," said Reggie, "What a fabulous view."

Robin was rather pleased he hadn't gone off on a long discourse after all, as it was quite clear that his passenger wasn't particularly interested in the details! "And why on earth would he be?" Robin asked himself rhetorically, "He's absolutely right. Never mind the geography lesson, why not just enjoy the scenery, the company and the gorgeous weather?" And he was of course, absolutely right!

Sitting up so high (for him) Reggie sort of thought of himself as a mahout, even though he knew it was very naughty and ungrateful (not least because it meant Robin was sort of his elephant!) to do so – especially as Robin had been so kind as to carry him!

By now they had reached the point where the sea wall turned the corner and not far ahead, they could see both the Boys and the Dog running each other ragged with chasing around and generally having a great time.

"This'll mean a monster lunch – nothing like a good walk with lots of fresh air to cultivate a big appetite," said Robin, who, from the look of glee on his face, certainly meant for him too as Reggie sussed at once! "We do this walk early evening if the Boys are staying over – cos they sleep like logs afterwards!"

Alex and Ian had both spotted their Dad and they waved excitedly.

They went into a huddle (kind of tricky with just two of them, but somehow they managed it!) and then, when they had hatched whatever stratagem they had been talking about, came running back along the sea wall.

When they reached where Robin and Reggie were at there was another quick round of whispers and then they both said together, "Will you carry me too?" This was rapidly followed by, "*Perleeese* Daddy," from both of them.

Everyone except Reggie, knew that this was not on — as even both Boys knew that they were way too big for Robin to carry them on his shoulders anymore.

Reggie looked slightly discomfited. He didn't want to spoil things for the Boys, but he really didn't want to get down — he was having far too good a time where he was!

"They're just teasing you Reggie; I haven't carried either of them for years."

As the realisation that he had been well and truly 'had' dawned, Reggie couldn't be cross, in fact the only thing to do was to laugh, so he did!

That made him nearly fall off though — which wasn't part of the plan at all!

"Gosh, a prank! That must mean they've accepted me!" That thought cheered him up even beyond the extremely cheerful mood he was already in — all his earlier nerves had long since disappeared and he was having a great time.

The rest of the walk passed without incident — it was all just such huge fun.

The Boys would race off ahead and Lettie would chase after them, bounce and wag for a while, and then come bounding back to Robin and Reggie as soon, and as often, as her doggie sense told her they needed herding or just checking on.

The only particularly noteworthy episode was when they were all on the way back and very nearly back at the Boat. A great big, lumpy sort of dog came lolloping up at them, barged past Alex and Ian (nearly knocking them over in the process) and stood itself in front of Lettie, sniffing at her. From some distance off Robin could hear a voice that seemed to be trying to call the dog away, but to no avail.

Meanwhile Lettie was being subjected to further attention — and, as she was doing everything she could to get out of the other dog's way, it certainly seemed that this interference was unwanted.

Eventually the dog's owner came on the scene, "I'm really sorry, he doesn't mean any harm, he's just friendly," she said.

Robin replied, "That's OK I suppose, no harm done."

Although Reggie could tell that Robin was about to say something else but that he had bitten it off before it could come out of his mouth.

The woman grabbed her dog by the collar and pulled him away from Lettie (with some difficulty it should be said as she was quite small and the dog was rather chunky!) and put his lead on. She then tugged him after her towards the car park where she pushed him into her truck-like 4x4.

"There really is no excuse for that you know, "said Robin, clearly annoyed, "She should have more control over that dog. It didn't, luckily, but, honestly, just about anything might have happened." He put his arms up and gently lifted Reggie off his shoulders, "What would have happened if you had been down there when that out of control bulldozer on legs came rushing towards us?" Before Reggie could answer him, Robin went on, "You could have been mauled and chewed up, that's what might have happened – let alone what it might have done to the Boys."

Clearly he was cross, so Reggie let him work it out in his own time. "There's no such thing as a bad dog, just bad owners who don't teach their charges the proper way to behave. Look at Lettie. Daft as a brush she may be, but she comes when she's called and doesn't mess with other people." Robin smiled, "Sorry, rant over; but it's just as well it didn't…." his voice trailed off into nothing.

Clearly he felt he had said enough – and he probably had!

This all went straight into the Bear's 'Note to Self' file with a big asterisk by it!

While this was going on the Boys and Lettie, all of who had recovered from the surprise that the other dog's arrival had caused, had made their way onto the jetty and were waiting, patiently (for them!), for Robin to let them in.

After opening the door and watching Alex, Ian and Lettie get onboard safely, Robin put one foot on the jetty, leaving one on the Boat, and gave Reggie his hand to help the Bear embark. "Hmmm," he said, "I think we need to do something about this." Despite a quizzical, "what do you mean?" glance from Reggie he said nothing else – because he was too busy making sure that the 'clean yourselves off before going into the Saloon' routine was being scrupulously observed!

"Right troops," said Robin.

Bear, Boys and Dog all stopped what they were doing and paid attention – it had been said in *that* sort of tone of voice! "Boots off, wash up, shoes on and back here in five to go to lunch. Not you Lettie, you stay here otherwise they'll never get themselves sorted out!"

The Dog stopped heading in the direction of into the Boat interior, and obeyed the command given, flopping down in the corner to await the return of her Chaps (various) and the Bear.

As lunch was in the offing it took the Boys next to no time to get organised. Only a few minutes went past before they were back in the Wheelhouse ready to be checked for going out to eat.

When they were all assembled Robin (who had, despite his size, managed to get ready in between the other three) said, "Right then, off we jolly well go."

And off they jolly well went!

To Reggie's surprise Lettie came with. "I hope you aren't leaving her in the car," he whispered to Robin, while pointing at Lettie.

"Of course not you daft Bear, that would be cruel." Robin seemed genuinely upset that Reggie should have thought that he would do that. "She is well known in the pub we are going to and is always well behaved, which is probably why she is welcome." He looked at her and continued, "And let's face it, she really is fabulous, who could fail to fall for those googly eyes and floppy ears."

Almost as if she had been given a prompt, Lettie looked up – heart meltingly so – and then slightly spoilt the effect by getting waggie!

"We're going somewhere else after lunch so we'll be going to the pub in the car."

Robin had to raise his voice to get the attention of Alex, Ian and Lettie – who had all started off at pace towards what they all knew to be the direction of the 'Black Dog' (which was, appropriately, the name of the pub).

Back they all trotted and dutifully got into the car – the Boys in the back seats and Lettie taking up most of the floor under their feet.

"Reggie, I have the Boys' old child seat for you to sit in. You need to be belted in by law and for safety's sake anyway, irrespective or whether or not anyone can see you."

This did not meet with Reginald Arbuthnot Cholmondeley's approval; not the being belted in bit (he thoroughly approved of both safety and obedience to the law!) but the 'being in a child's seat' bit was simply not on – so he made his feelings known.

Robin, in his best 'please don't argue with me, just do it' voice said, "It really makes much more sense, plus it'll lift you up so you can see out better."

In his best 'No, I am not having this' voice Reggie replied, " I am sorry Robin, but the car seat is not acceptable."

As he was *so* not in the mood for an argument Robin just said, "OK, you can sit between the Boys and use the lap belt then."

Although it appeared that Robin had caved, in fact he was right and Reggie was left to rue the result of his immature knee jerk reaction to the words 'child seat', as he was stuck between the rock of admitting Robin was right and the hard place of wanting to change his mind!

In his head, though, Reggie filed this as the 'Great Car Seat Debate' – and he counted it a win. Silly Bear!

With everyone properly secured in the car they took the short trip to the pub for lunch that was very much enjoyed by all and was indeed, as huge as Robin had predicted it would be!

After they had eaten they all waddled (yes, they had eaten *that* much!) out to the car and ensconced themselves in it again. When Robin had satisfied himself that everyone was secure, off they went.

It was only on this slightly longer trip in the car that the full extent of his earlier silliness became clear to Reggie. He could only see the sky and the occasional tree and, more to the point, the Boys were not quite as well behaved in the car as they had been on the Boat, during their walk or in the pub. Almost immediately they set off bickering and minor daftness ensued!

Robin naturally, was too involved in concentrating on the road and his driving generally to be bothered all that much with what was going on in the back – although he did, when it interrupted his focus, make the odd comment such as, "Please stop that." This had an immediate effect – but one that only lasted for moments before further usually different stuff started up!

"*Bother and toffee apples,*" thought Reggie, "Still I've made my bed, well my seat, so I have to sit in it I suppose." And he was absolutely right!

After a mercifully short (for Reggie) drive they arrived at their destination – a DIY superstore. The Boys both told him that car park was chock-a-block (Reggie couldn't see for himself) but as they went on to say in a weird two person speaking as if they were only one way "That's no problem because Daddy has a Parking Fairy." Sure enough, and before Reggie could ask for clarification, a parking space opened up right in front of them, the previous occupier choosing that precise moment to leave.

"See," said Robin (who had heard what the Boys had told the Bear), "it works every time – she's brilliant!"

Reggie decided it was better to go with it rather than to ask any questions and possibly break the spell.

The shop was crazy busy, "First nice day of springtime brings them all out," said Robin, in a tone that acknowledged that he accepted that the 'them' applied to him as well!

Robin bought a strange array of stuff – some fork handles (much to the Boys' relief – they had heard it many times before - he didn't do the joke about it sounding like 'four candles'), three small pieces of aluminium cladding, a large rubber bath mat, a couple of rubber walking stick ends and various coat hooks. After paying Robin shooed them all back to the car (they had left Lettie in it this time – with the windows open a bit – as Robin knew they would only be a few minutes and she preferred that to being tied up outside a shop) and off they went back to the Boat.

Alex and Ian were unusually subdued on the way back – they were both desperately trying to work out what on earth their Father was going to do with the things he had purchased.

Reggie was equally thoughtful.

None of them could work it out.

This was exactly as Robin planned it – he wanted them to wait so that they would be surprised and enthusiastic, when he revealed his plans.

When they got to the Boat Robin told them what he had in mind – they were going to build a ladder for Reggie to use to get in and out of bed and also a gangplank to allow him to get on and off the Boat on his own safely.

Obviously Reggie was chuffed with this and the Boys were excited that they were to be allowed to help with the constructions.

Robin explained what the various bits were for. "I am going to use the fork handles to make the ladder. Two of them for the sides and the other two, cut into bits, for the rungs. The walking stick ends go on the bottom to stop it slipping on the deck. Then two hooks at the top to hold it solidly on the bed."

He went on, "By fixing the aluminium cladding pieces together we'll make a gangplank. The rubber bath mat gets stuck onto it so as to avoid slipperiness when it gets wet as it is bound to do! Finally more hooks on either end to hold it on the jetty and the Boat."

As Robin went on board to get the tools he needed. Alex, Ian and Reggie exchanged looks and all of them grinned like crazy people; this sounded like a great fun way to spend the afternoon. And they were right – it was!

Robin came back out and gave instructions to the Boys as to which tools he wanted them to bring out for him (they were going to do the work on the jetty – to be near the electricity supply) and they duly complied.

There then followed an afternoon of tremendous fun.

For safety reasons they all had to wear goggles, and only Robin was allowed to use the power tools. There was the router (with which holes were cut in the fork handles and which also shaved bits off the rungs to make them fit in the holes that had been made) and the drill (which drilled holes for screws and bolts to go through to secure bits when they needed to be held together).

Actually Robin let both Alex and Ian have a go with his help at screwing screws into holes with the drill (which doubled as an electric screwdriver). They were also extremely helpful at holding things and getting the relevant bits at the relevant time.

In no time at all the odd assortment of bits and bobs had been transformed into a ladder and a gangplank.

"Slightly unusual looking, but I prefer to think of them as being unique; just like Reggie," said Robin when they had finished.

He put the gangplank in place and then walked across it, "I made it so if anyone is going to fall in the water cos it isn't solid enough it had better be me. Anyway if it takes my weight then it'll take just about anything!" Much to Robin's relief it was fine.

The ladder also worked perfectly – enabling Reggie to get on and off Robin's bed easily. After seeing this in place Robin said "Would you mind if Reggie used your room when you aren't here guys? That'll give us both a bit more privacy."

Without hesitation Alex and Ian both nodded. "Good, then he can use this then." With that, Robin produced a small hammock from behind his back!

Reginald Arbuthnot Cholmondeley was not entirely sure about this form of bed, but he was up for giving it a go!

Robin quickly fitted the last of the hooks and hung the hammock. It was only a little way off the ground so Reggie could get in easily (and so he wouldn't have too far to go before hitting the deck if he fell out!).

Warily Reggie sat on the hammock, and then swung his legs over and lay down.

"This is *really* comfy guys, but what do I use for covers?"

Robin pointed to a sheet and duvet which he had brought in and put on the lower bunk, "That," he said and the matter was settled.

"Right, teatime." No sooner had the words come out of his mouth than Robin was nearly bowled over.

Fortunately he was used to this sort of thing and was able to avoid the rush. He had deliberately made the announcement while Reggie was still in his swinging bed so as to make sure that he (Reggie that is) didn't get knocked down – a fact that didn't go unremarked upon by the Bear.

After tea – comprising scones, homemade jam and clotted cream, with squash for the Boys and tea for Robin and Reggie – they went for another walk, a shorter one this time as the time for Alex and Ian to leave was rapidly approaching (to everyone's disappointment, not to say sorrow).

It was on this walk that the only blot on an otherwise perfect day occurred when one of the Boys slipped on some mud and slid down a very grubby bank.

"Are you OK darling?" was Robin's first thought and question. "I'm fine, just very grubby Daddy, sorry," came back the answer to which Robin replied, in a very relieved tone of voice, "No worries. A little dirt never hurt anyone. We can cope with that. Just so long as you aren't hurt, that's the only issue."

It was only then that they all noticed that Reggie had, in trying to save the slippage, tripped over and fallen into a deep (in Bear terms) puddle – making himself all wet in the process.

That his tumble was second on Robin's list was not a matter of concern for Reggie he was only glad that no one had been hurt.

"Thanks for the effort Reggie, much gratitude and all that. Just as well we're pretty much at the Boat."

Robin could see the Bear wasn't hurt and he really did appreciate the attempt Reggie had made to save his son. "When we get in just strip everything off and we'll get you dry."

That, as it turned out, was considerably easier said than done and actually took an enormous amount of time and effort, but we'll draw a veil over the details!

Back at the Boat Robin got both Boys (and Reggie) to strip off in the Wheelhouse – with the former then changing into 'going home' kit – so as to avoid the considerable amount of muck that came off them from getting into the Saloon and beyond!

Their grubby stuff was neatly packed into plastic bags ready to be washed later.

It was dark by now, so when the Boys' Mother arrived to pick them up, the car's lights gave them plenty of warning.

Robin had made sure they had everything they had to go back with, and had packed their grubby clothes into carrier bags for later washing.

Then they were gone.

Reggie could see how sad Robin was when Alex and Ian had left so he just let his friend have a few quiet moments while he continued drying himself off.

"Right then, work tomorrow. How about some hot chocolate and the rest of the scones, then off to bed?"

Reggie agreed this was a really good plan.

"I'd like to wait until tomorrow to use my new hammock to sleep in if you don't mind," said Reggie.

They both knew that he was being thoughtful and offering companionship because Robin was sad – and Robin very much appreciated it.

"No problem, use the new ladder, eh?" and that was all that needed to be said.

CHAPTER 4

Reginald Arbuthnot Cholmondeley woke up. By now he was both used to, and very comfy with, both his surroundings and the circumstances, so there was only the normal confusion that almost everybody gets in that split second between being asleep and awake, which was very quickly completely dispersed.

He had been on the Boat with Robin for nearly a month now and they had easily and quickly got into a routine (but they were most definitely *not* in a rut!).

Things were moving ahead apace with Robin's 'crafty plan' and, although it wasn't moving as fast as Reggie would ideally have liked, there was definite and noticeable progress. In the meantime he felt like he really belonged and he, Robin, Alex, Ian and Lettie were getting on famously.

Once he had got his bearings Reggie realised he was grinning inanely. Luckily, he could tell Robin was still spark out (he could hear the snoring through the wall!) so there was no chance of anyone seeing quite how gormless his expression was! He glanced at the calendar on the wall and in a stage whisper, said, "Yes, today's the day for the big outing."

. . . . . . Just after tea the evening before, while they were sitting listening to some music, Robin had asked Reggie if he (the Bear that is) wanted to come with him (Robin that is) the next day (meaning the day in which the Bear had just woken up) as he (Robin again) was going on a special visit for work and had thought that Reggie would probably enjoy going with him to where he (Robin again) was going – Lords Cricket Ground in St John's Wood, London.

"I know you like cricket Reggie," Robin had said, by way of explanation, "and as I have to go chat to some people about getting tickets for U Support to give some disadvantaged kids the chance to get to go to the odd game there, it occurred to me that you might like to have a little excursion and come with. There's actually a game on – actually it's the final of the Minor Counties T20 competition, Devon versus Norfolk – so you can watch the start of the game while I have my meeting."

He paused to see if the idea met with approval and when he saw that it clearly did said, "I set the meeting so I can watch most of the match too."

Reggie was definitely up for the expedition as he didn't get to go out during the week very much – but going up to London, actually getting to go inside Lords *and* seeing some cricket sounded like the totally perfect day.

In his head Reggie paused to see if there was a 'catch', which there sort of was – and it followed on almost straight away after the stuff he was so excited about!

"The weather has finally changed for the better so we'll be going on the Triumph. That way we avoid the traffic, parking problems and the congestion charge all in one – result!" Robin beamed and went on, "Not forgetting what a total blast it'll be!" Reggie knew how much Robin enjoyed riding his motorbike – but only from what he had been told as the weather had definitely not been consistently biker friendly since he had been on the Boat.

The trip to London was to be Robin's first time out on it this year! The cause of Reggie's slight apprehensiveness (edging towards major panic attack!) was that, not only hadn't he been on Robin's Bike before he had never actually been on *anybody's* motorbike before!

As Reggie discovered later that same evening, the motorbike was definitely a 'him'.

Robin had taken Reggie to the garage where he was stored to get him ready for the next day's trip. To make sure 'he' stayed happy and ready for action when the time came, he had been kept safe and snug in his winter quarters, hibernating over the winter.

The Bike was a Triumph Trident 750cc naked muscle motorbike (which just means having no fairings or a windscreen) who was, naturally, British Racing Green – which was, as Robin made *absolutely* plain, "The only proper colour for a British motorbike."

Robin had also explained that he was called TW because he had a voice just like an American singer who Robin really liked.

Reggie liked the music too, although he wasn't quite as fond of this chap's stuff as Robin was, but he hadn't said anything about his ambivalence towards part of the catalogue because his Human was such a fan! Having listened to a lot of it though Reggie was certainly able to understand how apt the name was because when Robin had started him up after his winter break the Bike roared emphatically (which made Reggie actually leave the floor in a jump!) and then rumbled away with a low growl – which unquestionably bore a more than striking similarity to the voice of the singer in some of his songs.

When he first heard the news about the trip Reggie's head had conjured up a bubble of exhilaration that had expanded rapidly as he got more and more excited.

When however, the fact that they were going on the motorbike was mentioned the bubble wobbled about wildly, took on a completely different shape and very nearly burst as his brain processed the information it had received about the mode of transport they were to take.

As Reggie had never been on Robin's motorbike he was just a teensy weensy bit nervous (whilst also being really, really excited too!) about the whole upcoming experience. . . . . .

So here he was, on the morning of the trip, still not entirely sure about the day (well, he was certain he was going to love visiting Lords and watching the cricket – but he was still in two minds about riding on the bike).

Reggie knew that Robin would be waking up soon, because they had to leave quite early and the alarm had been set for a time when it would still be dark. That time was fast approaching – in fact it was going to be any second now!

He got out of his sleeping bag and made his way into the Saloon.

Reggie heard the sound of music coming from the Cabin. He counted down – 5, 4, 3, 2, 1 – Lift Off!

Robin didn't exactly emerge on cue (which might have spoilt the moment if Reggie hadn't have been so excited that he hardly noticed) but he did come through into the Saloon about seven seconds later and he was rubbing the sleep out of his eyes.

When Robin spied Reggie waiting for him he said, "Hello there Reggie, what are you doing up? I was expecting to have to drag you from your pit. You do know what time it is, don't you?" Robin paused right there as if he wasn't entirely convinced that *he* knew exactly what time it was and then said, "Well, whatever the time is it's still dark and that means that it's really far too early to be up and about."

At this Reggie looked a little (or even completely) crestfallen as Robin who despite appearances to the contrary was actually wide awake, noticed the Bear's expression, rushed to assuage any potential upset by saying, "Don't panic, Reggie! It was just a joke, of course I know why we've had to get up at this ghastly hour – we're off to Lords on the Bike!"

Robin had such an infectious grin that Reggie couldn't be cross with him for the prank, in fact he joined in with the laughter that Robin's grin turned into.

All of a sudden, as it dawned on him that they truly *did* have to get a move on, Robin switched from 'slightly dopey, not quite awake' to 'business-like and efficient'. Up to this point in their relationship Reggie hadn't seen such a metamorphosis from Robin, who was usually pretty laid back about most things – so he was shocked, but then impressed as Robin said, "Right, action stations, all hands to the wheel, noses to the grindstone and other bits to whatever seems to be appropriate." This bit of nonsense was much more like the laid back person Reggie knew and he relaxed – but only momentarily.

Robin continued, "Reggie, you need to get your stuff ready. I'll put the kettle on for some washing water for you. Please be careful turning off the gas – make sure it's completely off – and don't use all the water as I will want a cup of tea when I come back." With that he took the kettle, filled it with water and put it on the hob, which he lit.

Before the Bear could ask, Robin went on. "Lettie, come on girl, you're with me." He then picked up the plastic bag that was on the work surface next to the sink, slipped into his shoes, opened the door to the Wheelhouse (at which point Lettie did her normal squeeze past routine) took his jacket off the peg and grabbed the dog's lead. As he was undoing the padlock to the outside door he looked back at Reggie. "As we're going to be away all day I'm taking Lettie to Barbie's, who looks after her so she won't be lonely. Then, on my way back, I'll have a shower etc. When I return I need you to be pretty much ready to go. I laid out some stuff on the sofa for you last night to wear today.

At this Reggie looked over at the sofa and sure enough on it was a neat pile of clothes.

"See you in a bit then." And with that Robin was off – preceded by Lettie, who had, as always, managed to exit before anyone else! It was only then that Reggie became conscious that he had noticed that Robin was already dressed in his 'floppies' and not his nightclothes.

"Well I probably have quite a while, but better to be waiting ready than be the cause of any delay." Reggie was still a bit in shock from the imposing, 'business-like' Robin he had just seen and definitely didn't want to get on his wrong side!

While the kettle was heating up, Reggie went over to the sofa to look through the pile of clothes.

There was a pair of heavy-duty brown cords, a plain white tee shirt and a plain green sweatshirt – but there was also a pair of thick socks big enough to go all the way up and over his knees.

"Hmmmm, well I suppose Robin knows what he is about." Reggie hoped this was the case, as he couldn't see why he had to put socks on given the natural furriness of his feet.

While he was thinking about this the kettle commenced whistling (which meant it was just about boiling), so he turned off the gas under it (being, as he been told, very careful to make certain it was completely off) and climbed up the stepladder stool to the sink and went through his washing routine.

When Reggie was done he got dressed (he had made sure there was still enough water in the kettle for Robin's cup of tea!).

Even though he was still a bit confused as to why Robin had given him socks he put them on under the trousers.

He got up onto the sofa and opened his book to wait for Robin's return.

Reggie came to with a start. "Blast, I really have to stop dropping off on the chair like that."

He still had his book in his hands ("Phew, not lost my place then.") and hadn't moved from the position he had adopted on the sofa to read.

Robin had come into the Saloon. It was his arrival that had woken Reggie up.

"You all ready then, Reggie?"

Robin asked as he lit the gas under the kettle.

Making a mental note about how glad he was that he had decided to get ready straight away, Reggie replied, "Certainly, bring it on." This was an expression he had picked up from the Boys – which *he* thought made him sound very 'with it' (it was a shame he didn't know that using 'with it' was a sign that sadly he actually wasn't!).

"Did you put the socks on?" Reggie was glad that Robin had raised that as he felt it might be a little 'off' for him do so.

Still, now that it was out there he felt OK about asking stuff, "Yes," he said, "but why do I need them?"

"I thought you'd ask that. Going on the Bike isn't like going in the car. You're completely exposed to the elements, specifically the wind and even though it is Spring and apparently going to be sunny, it will still get pretty jolly freezing if you aren't properly wrapped up. I know you have furry feet but I thought the extra layer of sock would help keep you cosy. Better to have them on and be a little warm than have chilly tootsies and wish you hadn't left them here!"

Now while this made perfect sense, it had an effect on Reggie's bubble of excitement (which had been growing since he woke up). It made it have conniptions - again!

Now with a cup of hot, sweet tea in his hand Robin made his way into the Cabin to get dressed himself.

In no time at all he was back, dressed in a similar fashion to Reggie.

"OK Reggie – are you ready for this?"

Frankly Reggie was still unsure – but, as he was a great believer in the maxim 'Nothing ventured, nothing gained', he replied, "Absotively," he said – which was a ghastly miscoupling of two words that both the Boys and Robin used and which he had been unable to stop himself using, "let's do this thing!"

"Right," said Robin, "but first we need to sort out how you are going to be a pillion and then I want to make sure that you are totally *au fait* with the safety rules."

There was no doubting the seriousness with which Robin, rightly, took the latter and Reggie edged forward on the seat to show he was paying special attention – which he definitely was!

Robin noted the change in Reggie's demeanour and nodded appreciatively.

"Firstly it is imperative that you realise that riding a motorbike is potentially dangerous and not to be undertaken lightly or without careful preparation and the correct equipment. But that doesn't mean you shouldn't do it – as long as you follow the rules and take all the precautions you can to lessen the hazards. First here is a leather jacket for you to wear." He pointed to one of the dining chairs, over the back of which was a very smart, dark grey leather jacket. "It's Ian's – I cleared you borrowing it with him."

("Note to self," thought Reggie, "thank Ian.").

Reggie slid off the sofa, walked over to the chair, took hold of the jacket and put it on (with some difficulty – it was quite heavy!).

It was a little big, but he felt safer and therefore less nervous just from the weight of the material.

He looked quizzically at Robin, who explained, "It has Kevlar bike armour in – shoulders, elbows and back. That's what makes it so heavy, but that is also what will protect you if, heaven forbid, you come off."

Robin went on, "Next is the helmet. Not only is wearing it a legal requirement, it is also a very sensible safeguard."

He handed Reggie a child's motorbike helmet (it belonged to one of the Boys – as did the jacket, but the owner of it was the other one).

"This belongs to Alex – but I also cleared it with him."

("Note to self," Reggie thought again, "thank Alex.")

Reggie tried it on. Although he felt a smidge claustrophobic to start with, that soon passed.

"Great Reggie – you look every bit the Cool Biker Bear Dude," Robin commented.

It was a little tricky to hear with the helmet on – but Reggie heard that!

Then he did take it off to hear the rest of what Robin had to say by way of instructions.

"Finally there is the question of how we can actually carry you on the Bike."

Robin paused. He obviously had something to say that he was a little nervous about saying. He obviously decided to just bite the bullet and say it!

"Sorry Reggie, there isn't an easy or tactful way of saying this." Steeling himself for a possibly negative reaction to what he had to say, Robin took a deep breath and continued, "Your legs are too short to reach the foot pegs."

As a pragmatist, Reggie knew this to be the simple truth so he said nothing and Robin carried on, "I am going to have to carry you on my back in this."

Robin then produced the sort of contraption that parents use to carry small children in.

It was basically a backpack with a big hole in the top for the head and two holes each in the side and bottom for arms and legs.

It was hardly a dignified mode of transport for a Viscount – or anyone else!

Notwithstanding this, Reggie who was nothing if not practical said, "Clearly there is no other way Robin, so thank you for thinking of it."

Reggie also remembered what he thought of as the 'Great Child Car Seat Debate' which Robin had allowed him to win ("Yes," he thought, "I know I got my own way, but Robin was very reasonable and he had the Boys to contend with so I must be honest and acknowledge that it was me being given it rather than actually winning."). He also had to admit that Robin had actually been right about the car seat thing, so he probably was going to be right about this too. Finally it was, as well, undeniable that his feet wouldn't reach the pillion pegs – no matter how hard he stretched them!

Gathering up his own leather jacket (a black one that Reggie thought was well worn and *very* cool), helmet and a bag, Robin said, "Right, let's go then."

And after switching every off and locking up the Boat, that's what they did.

The first task was to dry the Bike off – it was still dark and the dew had settled overnight. Robin put his bag in the top box on the back, got a towel out of it and wiped all the relevant surfaces – including the seats, mirrors and controls.

Reggie could only stand expectantly and wait until this was done. After all he didn't want Robin to get a wet bottom!

Robin put the towel and his bag away, turned round and said,

"OK Reggie, put your scarf and gloves on and do up your jacket."
Reggie looked embarrassed, "Sorry Robin I must have left them inside." Then he remembered that Robin hadn't told him to bring a scarf – and he didn't have any gloves!

"Boo Yah!" Robin laughed at the prank he had played on his friend, rather unfairly as it was still very, very early. He produced a scarf and a pair of gloves from behind his back and gave them to Reggie saying, "You can use these, Alex's gloves and Ian's scarf – they said it was fine if you borrowed them."

Of course Reggie couldn't be cross after this, and he laughed out loud (and he also added the loan of gloves and scarf to the previous 'notes to self').

This was exactly what Robin had been hoping for; Reggie was completely disarmed and, as a result, was not worrying about going on the back of the Bike anymore – result!

"We're leaving this early so that we avoid most of the rush hour traffic. I'm going to go up the motorway, but we'll probably come back the 'pretty route'. You'll thank me (and the Boys) for the scarf, socks and gloves before we're done, believe me! And try to relax, you'll enjoy it much more if you do."

Once he was fully dressed (including his helmet) Reggie stepped into the carrier and Robin hefted it onto his back and got onto TW. There followed a certain amount of undignified (well as far as Reggie was concerned it was) adjustment of straps and general fiddle faddling about until Robin was satisfied that it was secure on his back.

"Are you sitting comfortably?" he asked.

"Yes." Much to his surprise Reggie actually felt both comfy and safe. His head, shoulders and arms were outside the carrier, with his legs sticking out of the holes made for that very purpose.

The die was cast and they were ready to go.

"One more thing before we set off Reggie. On no account move about in there without letting me know you need to please as, if you do, it will affect my balance and balance is the one thing that you very much need on a two wheeled vehicle. If you feel you have to move for any reason, tap me on the left shoulder twice, wait a couple of seconds and as I will then know that you are going to shift about, I can be ready to make allowance for it."

"Got it, twice on left shoulder if I need to move about."

"Cool beans." This was one of the expressions that Robin had picked up from the Boys that Reggie knew meant 'OK good stuff'

"Though why he can't just say that I don't know!" Reggie thought a bit grumpily to himself.

"Oh yes, and put the visor down to avoid the wind in your eyes," Having given Reggie this last piece of advice Robin opened the choke and pressed the starter.

The Bike roared into life (Reggie was ready for it this time!) and was clearly raring to get going.

"Right, off we jolly well go," shouted Robin (Reggie couldn't hear him of course but he got the idea). Robin clicked the lights on and put the Bike into first gear, then he gently let the clutch out and they started moving.

Off they were jolly well going!

Inside his head a little voice said to Reggie, "Don't forget to breathe," which was just as well as the Bear realised he was holding it in! "I'll get round to opening my eyes in a bit," Reggie said to himself.

The ground they were travelling over in the Marina was mostly small pebbles so Robin was going very slowly, keeping his legs off the pegs in case of slippage. They negotiated their way safely across to the exit where Robin stopped and looked three or four times, both left and right and then moved the bike out onto the road. Then he accelerated closing then opening the throttle and shifting up through the gears as their speed increased. Reggie's primary focus was still on remembering to breathe so he didn't have time to be either frightened or nervous as the pace rose. He still had his eyes shut too – he wasn't quite ready to open them just yet!

Although it seemed like ages to Reggie it actually was only a couple of minutes before he passed through the 'oh dear, this is scary' stage (which was only in his head) and realised that, far from being cause for nervousness or anxiety, this was really rather fun. He did maintain a degree of trepidation though – which was probably a good thing as it made him concentrate on not moving around in the backpack.

Of course he didn't *need* to move as physically he was snug and comfy but fidgeting is a natural, albeit unconscious, consequence of your mind trying to impose on your body, the view it has of the situation when they aren't on the same page of the reality book!

Satisfied that the act of regular breathing could now be safely left in the hands of his body's normal automatic pilot Reggie forced his eyes to open. He could tell that his mind was still suggesting that this would be a mistake – but he chose to ignore it!

Much to his intense relief (his brain was itching to say, "I told you so!") he found that having his eyes open made the whole thing considerably easier to cope with as he could see where they were going (his head was just far enough above Robin's shoulders to let him do this) and what they were going through and past. He felt a great deal more in control of the situation and this brought about the complete dissipation of all the stress and tension that still remained in his head. Even his mind acknowledged this – albeit grudgingly!

There was little or no traffic about as they made their way through the village towards the main road, indeed they saw practically no other vehicles until they got onto the motorway about fifteen minutes later, and even then there wasn't much. By then Reggie was much more relaxed and he was beginning to enjoy the whole thing tremendously.

They had, as Reggie found out later (he couldn't see the speedometer), been going quite slowly (apparently only thirty or forty miles per hour) until they got to the motorway (Robin always stuck to the speed limit – well near to it anyway). When they reached the blue motorway signs though things changed – Robin opened the throttle and TW roared ("Is it my imagination, or is that an 'exultant' noise," Reggie thought) and raced off up the road.

By now they were doing seventy (and a little bit!) miles per hour.

Once he had persuaded his heart to go back where it lived and leave his mouth (it had leapt in there after the initial burst of speed) Reggie become conscious that this was even more fun than it had been before.

The Bike felt totally stable and the sheer rush of slicing through the air was intoxicating. It was then that he understood how truly grateful he was for the socks, scarf and gloves as, great fun though it undoubtedly was cutting through, at speed, what he already knew was pretty chilly air definitely required extra layers over and around his furry body and appendages!

"Note to self, definitely do *not* forget previous 'notes to self' about thanking the Boys for the loan of their stuff, and add Robin to that list for suggesting that I use them." Reggie was not the sort of Bear to forget a service especially one that was so helpful!

They had been 'vrooming' along on the motorway for about twenty minutes when Reggie started to feel a little cramp starting to manifest in his left leg. He was just about to give it a wiggle to make the feeling go away when he remembered what he had been told so he tapped Robin twice on the left shoulder, counted to three and only then stretched his leg out.

What he wasn't ready for was what seemed like an immense force hitting his leg as it came out from behind Robin's back — it was the air rushing past the Bike. Reggie thought it was about to tear his leg off!

Naturally this was just hyperbolic twaddle conjured up in Reggie's head but it certainly caused a substantial shock to his system.

In actual fact his leg didn't move very much at all, other than the little shake he gave it to get rid of the cramp which worked just fine.

"Whoa; I am so glad I have Robin taking all this windiness for me," he thought.

A short while later Robin pulled in to the motorway services and stopped. "This is just on halfway to London Reggie," he said over his shoulder, "I usually stop here to stretch my legs and go to the loo whether I need to or not."

He paused while he loosened the straps and carefully lowered the backpack with Bear inside to the ground. "It isn't pleasant coping with the traffic when you are bursting to go. I call it a 'precautionary wee!" He looked questioningly at Reggie and then carried on, "I get the Boys to do it in circumstances like these, and they are cool with the concept." Clearly he was asking Reggie if *he* needed to use the facilities – or more correctly, he was hinting that the Bear really should.

"I'm fine, thank you Robin," said Reggie, "You go, I'll wait here by TW and have a stretch as you suggested."

"Well, if you're sure," Robin obviously wasn't convinced that Reggie had quite understood what was coming up, "It will take us a least another hour and a half before we get another opportunity."

"No problem, I can wait if I have to. I won't, but it'll be cool." Reggie was pretty sure he would be OK but he viewed this as a challenge so he was determined not to let his bladder let him down. Then as a way of changing the subject, he said, "By the way thank you very much for persuading me to wear the socks, scarf and gloves. This is great fun but I would have been a tad frozen without them."

"You're most welcom, Reggie. Couldn't have you uncomfortable could we otherwise you might not have been up for trips on TW in the future, and that's not to be contemplated."

Reggie was pleased at this, he was totally enjoying the ride and was chuffed to nuts at the implication that this wouldn't be the last time they did it.

Robin wandered over to where the shops and toilets were, leaving Reggie to decide whether to get out of the backpack or just to walk around with it on – which he could do, of course, because his legs were sticking out of it!

"I'm in it, so I may as well stay in it." And with the choice made Reggie went for a short walk. This turned out to be just around the Bike a few times as it was quite a bit more difficult to perambulate in the carrier than he had imagined it would (but still easier than getting out of, then back in, it!

Goodness only knows what the few adults who were milling around thought as they saw a Bear, not only walking, but doing so in a backpack while at the same time wearing socks and a motorbike helmet! Clearly though they were all too grown-up to let the actual reality intrude on their individual consciousnesses as none of them gave him so much as a second (or even in some cases, a first) glance.

Reggie noticed this and not for the first time (nor was it likely to be the last) reflected sadly, that the world would be a much better place if people just got older but didn't grow up.

In no time at all they were back on the road and whizzing towards London. The sun was coming up and was creating a beautiful colour picture of the sky and land off to the right as they rode northeast towards the great metropolis.

As they got closer to London (Reggie could tell this from the signposts) the volume of traffic gradually increased.

Huge aeroplanes were regularly visible overhead. They appeared to be moving incredibly slowly, but Reggie knew this was just an illusion.

Reggie saw signs for 'Heathrow' with a white pictogram plane on them, "That must be where they're going," he thought – and of course he was right.

As the signposts changed from Blue to Green the road became a flyover passing between buildings on either side.

As they went past one structure with some model cows on the top of it, Reggie felt rather than heard Robin speak.

Obviously with all the noise of the wind rushing past he couldn't catch the actual words but later when he asked about it, Robin explained, "When I was little, the same sort of age that my Boys are now, my Dad told me that this is where London starts – where the cows on the dairy are. Frankly I am not convinced that it's *actually* true but it's close enough so I've passed it on to the Boys. Whenever we come up this way we have a sort of tradition that the first one to notice the cows wins a little prize so it has become pretty much second nature to say it when we go past."

Reginald Arbuthnot Cholmondeley was all for traditions – even new ones – so he made a 'Note to Self' and being by nature a competitive Bear he vowed that next time he would try to win.

The Bike slowed from seventy, then to fifty and then to forty miles per hour as the road went from a high speed inter city motorway to suburban throughway.

With this change came another – loads of traffic!

As the road angled down to the ground and stopped being a flyover Reggie could see a roundabout up ahead and both lanes leading up to it were covered with cars, vans, lorries and a coach all just sitting there nose to tail.

"This is where the Bike really comes into its own," thought Reggie, as Robin carefully manoeuvred their way among the gap that was left between the inside and outside lanes by most of the drivers of the immobile four-wheeled vehicles.

Unfortunately there were some (and there always are!), utterly thoughtless and inconsiderate drivers who apparently wanted the whole road for themselves and had positioned their vehicle slap bang next to the white line separating the lanes.

When they came to the places where the gap was smaller, Robin slowed right down and either 'walked' the Bike through or just waited until the line moved. Usually to be fair, the thoughtless motorist recognised that there was a motorbike trying to get through and moved over a bit but occasionally, there were those who were just too selfish to do so – which meant Robin had to wait for a gap to open up. All in all though they made much swifter progress than they would have done in a car.

The surroundings changed from industrial to residential with, at one point, two sports stadia on either side of the road practically opposite each other.

From the signs Reggie worked out that the one on their left was Twickenham – headquarters of English rugby. "I'd really like to go there one day," Reggie thought – well saying it out loud (and expecting Robin to hear) was completely pointless in the current situation! Reggie was a fan of most sports but rugby and cricket were two of his favourites.

They crossed a bridge over a big river and then went past a huge park. The traffic had become a little lighter but this didn't last long as the road narrowed from two lanes to one. Negotiating this section was a bit trickier because Robin had to overtake and that necessitated crossing the white lane in the middle of the road, so they stopped more often to wait for the way ahead to be clear. This wasn't much of an issue though as it was obvious that the vast majority of the traffic was heading into and not out of central London.

"I see now why we left so early," mused Reggie, "it can only get worse as more people make their way to work."

He was absolutely right about that!

They were approaching a big junction with a small bridge over the top of the middle of the roundabout, which, as Reggie found out when they next stopped, this was called the 'rickety rackety bridge' (not really – it was another 'tradition' in Robin's family).

The name was most apt though. As they went over it you could hear 'rickety rackety' noises.

Apparently (at least this was what Robin's Father had told him, so Reggie completely understood why Robin accepted it as true) it had been put up decades ago as a temporary measure but had never been replaced.

Reggie was glad he hadn't known about it before they used it because frankly, it felt a little bit precarious!

Next they were on a dual carriageway again, passing through the middle of what Reggie presumed was a town (he was wrong as it turned out because it was actually Hammersmith, which is a Borough – Greater London is made up of lots of these).

On this bit they were doing forty miles per hour at the most – but only when road conditions and traffic allowed of course!

The road turned into a flyover, which Reggie found very exciting. He looked to his right and saw that the sun was finally in the sky – albeit very low down still. It was illuminating one of the prettiest of all the bridges that go across the Thames – Hammersmith Bridge.

From Hammersmith they drove through Earl's Court and then up towards Knightsbridge.

Before they got there Robin turned off to the left ("Oh, what a shame. I was rather hoping to see Harrods," thought Reggie) just past the main entrance to the Natural History Museum (which Reggie thought was a little bit OTT!) and then went up Exhibition Road, past the side of the Victoria & Albert and Science Museums on their right and left respectively.

At the top of the road they crossed over into Hyde Park.

"Gosh, this is nice," said Reggie out loud – effectively to himself of course as there was no way Robin was going to hear him.

Robin took the route straight through the Park, over the Serpentine and on towards the northern edge.

Once they were out of the park the only thing Reggie was able to recognise was Paddington Station ("Named after a famous Bear, naturally.") and then he got totally confused as Robin took lots of side roads.

It turned out that Robin had lived in this part of London for quite a few years while he was at Law School so even though there had been some changes (like new one way systems) he still was able to navigate through it pretty well.

Eventually their meanderings brought them out onto a big wide thoroughfare, heading north – at least that was Reggie's best guess, as the sun was behind and slightly to the right of them.

Crossing this big road by doing a quick left, then a right, they zipped up a leafy street until Robin slowed right down, stopped completely, and then carefully backed TW into a space in a parking bay marked 'Solo Motorcycles Only'.

Obviously they had arrived.

Robin got off the Bike and did the necessary to ease the backpack off and place the Bear carefully on the ground.

He took off his helmet and said, "Right, here we are then, did you like the trip?"

Reggie had loved almost every minute of it (during the bits he didn't he had just shut his eyes and trusted to Robin's riding skills!) so he had no problem in replying, "It was utterly brilliant!"

Robin beamed – he always got a big kick out of turning people onto riding.

"You see, you don't have to ride like an idiot to have a great time on a bike. Safety first, second, third and last I say."

With Reggie holding, then passing stuff to him, Robin put the helmets, gloves and the carrier in the top box.

"Pass me your jacket too Reggie," said Robin, passing him a fleece to wear instead.

"Thank you for thinking of that Robin," said Reggie (who was relieved at not having to wear the heavy biker jacket, cool though it was, all day).

Robin kept his jacket on and both kept their scarves on – there was a distinct 'nip in the air'.

Lastly Robin put the disc lock on TW (who Reggie could swear was 'purring'!) turned to Reggie and said, "Right, cup of coffee and a sticky bun possibly with real cream in, then off to Lord's. Do you approve?"

Reggie hadn't bargained for a drink and bun – but he wasn't about to pass them up! "Make mine a hot chocolate though please."

Then he remembered something, "Socks. I don't need those on anymore."

"Right," said Robin, "Up on the Bike with you, it'll make it easier to remove them."

And with that Robin lifted Reggie up and plonked him on the pillion seat. The Bear was a bit flustered, but saw the logic and proceeded to desock, handing them to Robin (who put them in the top box with the other stuff).

When Reggie was done and had been helped down off the Bike, Robin said, "Cool beans. Onward to sustenance!" And he started off in the direction, it must be assumed, of the café with a startled Reggie scurrying along behind, desperately trying to catch up.

Robin knew this would be the effect his departure would have and was just being a bit naughty – so he stopped to let the Bear reach him about ten yards along the pavement.

CHAPTER 5

Reginald Arbuthnot Cholmondeley woke up. He did so because he was being shaken, gently it has to be said, by the shoulder. "Come on Reggie snap to and finish your chocolate and bun; it's 9.15 and nearly time we were off to Lord's."

"*Blistering Bananas* did I drop off to sleep?" He had only meant to think this but his mouth tripped him up and it came out in real 'out there in the world' words!

130

Robin felt no need to answer however, as it was all too obvious that Reggie had nodded off in the coffee shop where they had each just finished (at least Reggie thought they had only just finished – but maybe it was little while ago? How long had he been asleep? He was mildly confused) a super cup of steaming hot chocolate (with chocolate powder and sprinkles – result!) and a hideously sticky, but utterly scrummy bun. Robin had gone with his original choice of coffee (a very large, very frothy cappuccino – also with chocolate powder on the top) but the net effect was the same.

Clearly the trip on the Bike (and all the consequent fresh air) had made Reggie drowsy. "Well I'm going with that as the reason," he said in his head as it was a little less embarrassing than the most likely real reason – that they had got up hideously early and he was a Bear that needed his sleep.

Robin was grinning, rather impishly, at him; clearly he knew the truth, but Reggie felt too good, replete with the drink and bun and still buzzing from sheer joy and the sense of exhilaration from the ride up to be bothered – and that was exactly how it should be.

Robin had already paid for the mini feast so they could just get up and go, so up they got and went.

"Lord's is only just round the corner Reggie, are you going to be OK walking?"

The Bear was too buzzed by the prospect of where they were going to be cross, or even moderately annoyed at the implication that he couldn't manage a short walk, so he just said, "Yes," and left it at that.

In fact it was exactly as Robin had said and so, no more than five minutes later, they were standing outside the famous Grace Gates – which had been named to honour the memory of William Gilbert (almost inevitably abbreviated to 'WG') Grace, the most celebrated English cricketer of the nineteenth century – if not of all time.

"This is the Members entrance Reggie. I was asked to wait just outside it for the Secretary of the Club, who I'm meeting."

Despite the fact that the match between Devon and Norfolk wasn't due to start until 11 a.m. (over an hour away) there were quite a few people milling about both inside and outside the ground. Some had furled banners, others were wearing silly hats, most were carrying cool bags or boxes, but all were dressed warmly against the chill early morning weather. The sun was high in the sky, well and truly shining and there wasn't a cloud in the sky, so that boded very well for the day and thus also the match.

Reggie noticed that there was a palpable, uniformly 'friendly' atmosphere, with opposing supporters mixing freely with each other chatting away happily. He remembered a maxim his Father had often used 'The Game's the Thing' and standing amongst this unmistakably amicable crowd, he finally got it!

"You're welcome to come into the meeting with me Reggie, but it'll probably be quite boring – cos you won't really be able to take part. Alternatively, you could just wander around, take in the ambience of the place and find us a spot to watch the game." He paused for thought and then went on, "My guess is that you'll get into the Pavilion without a ticket as they won't see you. I think if you can get in the Gate without being stopped that'll prove it."

"Sorry Robin, I'm not with you. Can you explain please."

"Well the Pavilion is the 'inner sanctum', the 'holy of holies' and you only get in if you can prove you are entitled to – either because you are a Member or if you have the appropriate Pass or ticket. I've wangled a Visitor's Pass that will get me in but only the one I am afraid – I couldn't think of a valid reason, well one that the Club would understand, to ask for two. Sorry Reggie."

"*Pas de probleme*," Reggie was picking up Robinisms, "What's the plan then?"

"The Guardians of the Pavilion and the Gate have always struck me, now that I have a reason to think about it, as being particularly grown up. My idea is that if you can walk through the Gate without being stopped you should be able to walk into the Pavilion as well. Then, when my appointment is done with I can meet you on the benches in front of the Pavilion down by the pitch. If I don't see you there then we'll watch from the Mound Stand – which is next to the Pavilion. How does that sound to you?"

It sounded entirely practical to Reggie and he said so, "Good plan Robin. Let's see how things go with getting in here, shall we?" And with that the Bear marched off through the Gate.

Reggie looked at the chap checking tickets and just *knew* he was very grown-up, so unsurprisingly, Reggie's presence wasn't even perceived as a tiny anomalous 'blip' on the radar – result! The Bear came back out – still nothing.

"Well that all seems to be in order, plan A then I think. Do you want me to wait here with you?"

"Very kind of you Reggie but you go off and have a look around. I expect to be finished by the time the match starts or very soon thereafter, so I'll see you on the Pavilion seating at about 11. If you aren't there then I'll look for you here, well, inside the Gate rather than outside it at 11ish. Is that cool?"

It was, and the Bear said so.

Things being organised Reggie walked through the Gate again and headed off into the ground for the start of the second instalment of his great adventure of a day.

As Robin waited for his host he watched his friend ("Yes," he thought, "definitely my friend, but so much more than that as well.") disappear into what was rapidly becoming more of a throng than simply a crowd.

He didn't have long to wait as very soon, he saw a man clearly very much at home in his surroundings coming towards him. When he was in comfortable talking distance the man said, "You must be Robin, how do you do, I'm Giles. We spoke on the telephone." This was, indeed, the man Robin had come to meet.

"Very pleased to meet you Giles. Do please accept my apologies again for the rather casual dress. I remembered a tie to get into the Pavilion though."

This brought a smile to Giles' face, "That's quite alright. I ride a bike too so I totally understand the attraction of using one to get here. How was the trip?" As he was talking Giles handed Robin his Visitor's Pass, a laminated card on a ribbon, for it to be hung around the holder's neck. Robin put it on as they made their way through the Gate – getting a smart salute as they did so.

"Great, thank you. Minimal traffic so a whiz up the M3, fairly easy journey from Twickenham on, no hassle parking, no congestion charge – pretty standard stuff really. It was brass monkeys of course, but that's all part of the fun isn't it?"

They both grimaced knowingly, and then both laughed at once, "Oh, and arrival timed to allow for a cappuccino and sticky bun round the corner before coming here."

Giles named a café and Robin replied, "Is there anywhere else worth going to for that around here?" and they laughed again! This was a good start to the meeting and augured well for a result Robin felt.

Reggie was having the time of his life. He had tried to get into the Pavilion ("Better check that out first.") and the result was exactly the same as it had been at the Gate ("Clearly Robin was right about the Guardians."), in and out again without so much as a sideways glance in his direction so that was sorted.

He had just over an hour to 'kill' before the match started and he met up with Robin again., although he didn't really like the expression to 'kill' time as he felt that time was a precious commodity which should never even be wasted let alone 'killed'. Of course what constituted a 'waste of time' was somewhat of a moveable feast; indeed there were some very flexible parameters operating with this, and frankly they were dependant solely on what sort of mood Reggie was in at the time but the basic principle was a sound one. Well that was his view and he was sticking to it! Anyway drifting round the Home of Cricket, even if done a little aimlessly, was in his humble opinion, most certainly not even close to being in the 'waste of time' category howsoever one looked at it.

Reggie had meandered all around the west side of the ground and ended up back at the entrance to the Pavilion. "I know, I'll check out the seating."

As he was a Bear that believed in forward planning, he went back in. There were a great many humans in a not very big space and Reggie was treated to a live demonstration of how grown ups deal with having a mobile, sentient Bear in their midst. Essentially they simply made room for him without as was clear from the occasional puzzled looks he noticed, understanding what it was, or who it was they were getting out of the way of!

This went straight into Reggie's 'Note to Self' file as he felt that it was of importance and should be remembered.

He made his way through the building and had no difficulty in finding what he was looking for, so he made a note of how to get there for later.

When he looked at the seating available to Members and Guests he was a bit taken aback. They were simple benches painted white and frankly, they looked truly uncomfortable!

"Just as well I carry my own seat padding!" Reggie was ready to acknowledge this as a fact (which of course it was), but he would never admit it to anyone else. Still, he was determined that nothing was going to spoil his day – not even that (he *did* like his comforts) – so he put it to the back of his mind.

Having found what he was looking for he went back out of the Pavilion and headed towards the shop, just to look, not to buy (well Robin had all the money.). Of course if he saw anything particularly noteworthy then it would be only right and proper that he draw Robin's attention to it – wouldn't it? Before he could get there he was brought up short by the sight of another Bear walking in through the Grace Gate. Fascinated and curious at this, his first sighting of another Bear, Reggie changed course and headed towards the new arrival to introduce himself and to find out who this other Bear was.

The other Bear saw Reggie approaching and realising they were on a 'collision' course, stopped to wait for him to arrive.

As he reached the other Bear Reggie said, "I hope I am not intruding, but I couldn't resist saying hello to a fellow Bear, especially as you are the first I've come across since I got my Human. My name is Reginald Arbuthnot Cholmondeley, how do you do." The other Bear was a good (Bear's) head taller than Reggie and he was, shall we say, of a rather more slender frame.

He was wearing a pair of very smart, very deep grey moleskin trousers and an emerald green cardigan with chunky black buttons.

"What a delight to meet you too. I'm Vivian Peter Langrish, but please call me Vivian, or Viv, as all my friends do."

As he said this he held out his paw.

Reggie took it and shook it saying, "Please, I'm Reggie all *my* friends call me that". He just *knew* that this was what the two of them were going to be.

"What brings you here then? Said Viv, "Apart from the cricket obviously."

"My Human is meeting the Secretary. He'll be coming to watch the game after that. I love cricket, so he suggested I come along. What about you, are you just here to watch the cricket?"

"My Human and I have some business in London to attend to but, as we actually live and work mostly in Exeter we couldn't pass up the chance to come and cheer on our local team. Have you come far?"

"From Emsworth, in Hampshire. We live on a Boat in the harbour"

Viv grinned, "What a small world! My Human, Michael, was born and brought up in Southampton – just up the road from you."

It was Reggie's turn to grin, which he did. "Smaller than you think Viv. *My* Human, Robin, is from Southampton and still works there. He only recently moved to Emsworth to live on his Boat full time."

Reggie became a little coy and went on, "I only got my Human, who is rather older than I was expecting, just after Easter and so all this is still a bit new to me. Of course I got the normal talk from my Father so I suppose I must have all the theoretical knowledge." (Now that I've remembered it," he said to himself).

Unnoticed by Reggie Vivian raised his eyebrows quizzically at this piece of information.

Reggie went on, "To be honest though I'm still finding my feet a tad on the practicalities. Also, I was starting to think I was the only Bear left – you're the only other one I've met so far."

As they were talking they were also walking and as Reggie recognised from his earlier explorations, they were heading toward the Pavilion – or more correctly, that was where they had now arrived.

Viv turned to Reggie and said, "Would I be right to take it that you and your Human intend to watch the game from here?"

"Oh yes, Robin has a Visitor's Pass for the day and as you must know, we can just walk straight in."

"Excellent." exclaimed Viv, " After you then." And they went in.

Viv, who clearly knew his way around, led them through the building by what Reggie acknowledged was a much quicker route than he would have taken and down to a section of the seating where there were a couple of coats and a cool box – and a Human!

Gesturing towards the tall, distinguished looking man sitting by the coats Vivian said, "Reggie, please allow me to introduce my Human. Michael Laurence Langrish, this is Reginald Arbuthnot Cholmondeley."

"How do you do Mr Cholmondeley, please call me Michael."

As he said this he stood up and held out his right hand.

Reggie took the hand in his paw and while shaking it said, "Very well, thank you for asking - but not 'Mister', please do call me Reggie, if you don't mind."

"Reggie's Human, Robin, has a meeting with Giles and will be joining us shortly," said Viv. Obviously they were well up on the Club hierarchy.

"Please sit here, Reggie," said Michael, moving one of the coats which they were using to reserve their places, "We'll save Robin a seat as well."

"Thank you very much, much appreciated." Reggie was in no doubt that, purely fortuitously, he had fallen on his feet!

He and Vivian sat down next to each other on the bench between the coats.

Before he could sit down again however, Michael saw someone he knew coming out of the door to the Pavilion. "Please excuse me chaps, there's a pal of mine over there and I need to talk to him – work stuff. I'll be back in a bit."

"Rightie Ho, see you soon Michael," said Viv, "Try not to miss the toss."

Giving both Bears a jolly little wave, Michael made his way along the row of seats they were in and made his way towards his friend.

All the way up he was secretly imagining himself to be in his pads coming back from the middle after scoring an unbeaten century to win the game; something he did every time he ascended the famous Pavilion Steps at Lord's.

Actually Vivian knew that his Human indulged in this fantasy – as he too had his own daydream when going up the steps; only his was that he had just taken all ten of the opposition's wickets! He had still won the game of course.

After Michael had left the two Bears started chatting again. Both of them felt, quite independently, on the sort of comfort level with the other as if they had been best buddies for years, so they had no qualms about the nature or scope of their discussions – anything and everything was on the table.

Obviously some of this arose from the innate sense of ursine fraternity but, beyond the species brotherhood aspect they just really instinctively liked each other!

Notwithstanding all of this however, Reggie was slightly nervous about raising the topic that was uppermost in his mind – something that he sensed his new chum could probably help him with, but which was on the fringes of the line that even best mates think twice (or even thrice) before crossing. This was, as I am sure you can guess, the matter of his name and title.

"No," he thought, "Robin has a great, not to say crafty, plan that is maturing nicely so let's not potentially spoil my new friendship by asking for a favour before we've really got to know each other. Anyway the day is not about me, it's about the glorious weather, the cricket and most wonderfully of all, new friends."

And having decided this, Reggie settled down to enjoy the day.

He looked at the sky and could see that it was definitely heating up and that the sun certainly had his hat on – and it was probably an MCC one at that!

"So Vivian, tell me about how you got your Human?" He paused as it crossed his mind that this might be one of those 'questions' that one simply didn't ask as fellow Bear, "Only if that's not too personal a question of course." He hoped that last bit would avoid any potential awkwardness.

Viv laughed out loud but it was, unmistakably, a nice friendly and companionable laugh, as, by its tone, Reggie could tell it was meant to be with, not at him.

"Don't panic my dear chap; not only is that a perfectly normal enquiry for us Bears to make, but quite often it is the question we ask when we first meet."

Reggie sighed a very relieved sort of sigh, "Thank goodness for that," he said, "I'm still a bit fuzzy on basic protocols. It's one thing to know, another to do."

Reggie's new friend smiled and said, "In fact, given that your Human is clearly an adult and you told me that you had only just got him, I was about to ask you the very same question. Your situation is, as I am sure you are aware, rather unusual and you have certainly piqued my curiosity." Before Reggie could answer Vivian went on, "But as you asked before me and as it is such a normal and socially acceptable question amongst us Bears, I am happy tell you my story first, especially as we have all day. We do don't we, you don't have to get back, do you?"

Reggie replied, "No, Robin sorted things so that we'd have time to watch the game together – and we don't have anything urgent dragging us back."

He hoped this was the case (it was) as he had remembered that Barbara was looking after Lettie and he didn't know when she was expecting the, or if it would be all right for them to be a bit late. "Well we are on Robin's motorbike so I presume he would prefer riding back in the daylight."

Apart from that though nothing could drag him back early.

He mentally crossed his claws as he thought this – but felt pretty safe, as he knew Robin loved cricket too and would most likely have cleared the Dog watching timing to cover it.

From his expression Reggie could tell that his new pal was very happy with the answer he had received.

Vivian gathered his thoughts and started his tale. "In point of fact I took over Michael from my Father, Edward, some ten years ago when he decided to retire from active duty – my Father that is. Up to then Michael had been his Human, but I helped out if required."

That you could 'inherit' a Human was news to Reggie and he said so to Vivian.

"Indeed, yes we can, actually it's quite usual. My Father still lives with us, that is Michael, his lovely wife and me, but he is really quite old now and to be honest, tends to spend most of his time reading, watching cricket and sleeping – although not necessarily in that order and not always at different times." A funny thought obviously flashed across Vivian's mind, "Don't tell my Dad or Michael, who still thinks the world of him, but I regularly catch him snoozing in front of a Test match on the television with a book in his hand." Once again Vivian laughed.

The laugh was so infectious that Reggie couldn't help joining in until he realised how rude that might sound. He stopped instantly, which unfortunately, provoked a fit of coughing instead!

Reggie fought for breath, but was able to splutter out an apology, "Gosh, I am so sorry Vivian, how rude you must think me laughing at your Father."

"Don't mention it m'dear it *is* funny (in a nice way) so laughter is exactly what is called for."

Reggie was finally beginning to feel much more relaxed and had stopped being such an old worry wart about offending Vivian (who was so evidently much more a 'Bear of the World' than Reggie was). "Cool beans, do please go on." he said. Nothing could be better evidence of his state of relaxedness than the use of one of Alex and Ian's idioms!

"Anyway, my Father got Michael when he (Michael that is) was a tiny baby – and yes I know, that's difficult to imagine when you see how tall he got, but he was tiny once – or so at least I am reliably informed. After the best part of fifty five years my Father felt he'd done his bit and he passed Michael onto me." Something clearly then occurred to Vivian and he said, "You may be wondering about my slightly unusual first name."

Reggie shook his head, "It hadn't even crossed my mind that it was unusual, in fact I think it's particularly cool."

"Thank you, I certainly think so." Vivian was evidently please at this because he beamed and then went on, "Well I was named for my Father's two favourite cricketers – Sir Vivian Richards of Somerset and the West Indies and Peter Sainsbury of Hampshire and the MCC. He loved the former for his sheer aggression and the power, grace and style of his batting and the latter for his loyalty and consistency. As a family we have always been stalwart Hampshire fans and Sainsbury was the only player to appear in both our County championship winning sides – in 1961 and 1973."

The source of his Christian names was plainly a matter of some pride for Vivian – with a great deal of justification Reggie thought.

"I have two sisters and a brother. I am the eldest – which is why I took on Michael. My sisters look after Michael's two daughters and my brother looks after his son. I also understand that at least two of Michael's grandchildren call my Father 'Grandpa Bear', which is sweet. Michael believes they are actually referring to him and naturally he loves it. We don't want to spoil his little illusion so don't spill the beans will you, there's a good chap."

"Wouldn't dream of it, our Humans do need lots of bolstering don't they."

Both the Bears guffawed loudly at this, which, as far as they were concerned, was a simple statement of fact.

"There you have it. That's my story Reggie. So what about your tale then? How on earth did you end up starting out with an *adult* Human?"

Before Reggie could answer Vivian added, "I presume that Robin is an adult as he rides a motorbike; although that of itself might be grounds for speculating that he wasn't very grown up." Both Bears tittered at this and Reggie nodded vigorously. Vivian continued, "Still even though he must be fully grown he can't be grown up as such. Frankly Reggie I am rather confused, but utterly fascinated. I can't recall this sort of thing ever happening before. "

Secretly Reggie was chuffed to nuts to have found something about himself that his friend was interested in. This is normal when you meet someone you like, admire and respect (as Reggie instantly did with Vivian), but that doesn't stop it being a little unworthy – and he knew it!

Reginald Arbuthnot Cholmondeley started at the beginning – being in the shop and being taken to the Boat by Robin's friend; and then went onto all the other stuff that you've already read about. Well, not *all* actually. He left out the part about his name being spelt wrongly – for the reasons he had decided on earlier – and having to get his name and title sorted out.

Naturally Vivian didn't actually notice any incorrect spelling of Reginald Arbuthnot Cholmondeley's surname, as the Bear had been spelling it properly when he used it ever since someone other than *his* Human had shown belief in him and his story – namely Barbara and the Boys.

"Bless my cotton socks!" said Vivian, who didn't actually wear socks as a rule but did on occasion use that expression, "That *is* a tale and three quarters and no mistake. As I said before, in my experience and I believe that of any other Bear, what you have taken on is unique in Bear History – and I am sure I don't need to tell you how long, varied and notable *that* is!"

Reggie was uncertain whether he should be proud, pleased, frightened, overawed or just plain gobsmacked! "Really?" was all he could muster in response – and that didn't begin to cover it!

Luckily for Reggie both Michael and Robin chose that moment to come down the Pavilion steps towards the Bears. Michael arrived first, followed in very short order by Robin.

What then happened was one of those bizarre mix-ups beloved of the makers of classic silent comedy, with Bears and Humans both making fools of themselves trying to introduce, be introduced, shake hands, say 'hello, please call me...' and similar stuff like that.

Robin and the Bears were inexplicably tangled up with each other, with no obvious signs of how that had happened or indeed, how they could extricate themselves.

Eventually Michael took charge by saying, "Right, I am Michael, this is Robin. Robin this is Vivian or Viv, and everybody has already met you Reggie." That settled, they got on with the business of getting to know each other and watching the cricket.

It transpired that they had all missed the toss; Reggie and Vivian because they were so engrossed in each other's stories and Michael and Robin because they hadn't concluded their business stuff. They brought themselves up to speed by asking one of the other people sitting in their vicinity what had happened.

They were told that Devon's Captain had called correctly and had chosen to field first, preferring to chase the runs apparently. As this piece of information was passed on Norfolk's openers started down the Pavilion steps to much applause from all parts of the ground.

"I don't know about you Michael, but I always imagine myself returning to a standing ovation having scored a century to win a vital Test from what was universally considered to be a totally unwinnable position," said Robin.

"Me too as it turns out, this place will do that to you, don't you think? So much history and tradition," replied Michael.

The Humans had clearly found a topic of conversation of mutual interest immediately.

Vivian looked at Reggie and winked – 'nuff said!

There was however, one thing that Reggie felt he should ask before they got down to the serious business of enjoying themselves, so he asked Robin, "How did it go? Did you get what you came for? Did you persuade the Club to give you any tickets for U Support?"

Robin's humungous grin would have been answer enough but he confirmed it by saying, "Better than I hoped actually – eight pairs (one for the child and one for his or her carer) of season tickets for all but the International games and the various Finals that get played here – a mega result! But let's not talk about it now, let's just take pleasure in the company and the surroundings."

This made sense to Reggie and the two of them turned back to their new friends and commenced to the matter at hand - getting on with the day.

From its auspicious beginnings through to the close of play, the rest of the day just got better – but went past in a blur of unmitigated delight for Reggie and his friends.

The match was generally enthralling but with enough lulls and breaks to allow for bonhomie and good comradeship to ensue amongst the four of them, of which there was plenty!

It turned out that Robin had only had his tie (necessary for him to get into the Pavilion as you will remember) and a thin file of work papers in his bag which had left plenty of room for sandwiches, crisps, sausage rolls, cheese and pickle buns and some apples and bananas.

"I made them last night while you were asleep." Robin explained to Reggie.

Obviously they offered to share the picnic with Michael and Vivian – but they of course had their own cool box with similar but subtly and interestingly different snacks and treats in, which they suggested be pooled with Robin and Reggie's to make a real banquet for the four of them – Result!

Consequently none of them went hungry (or thirsty – there was flavoured water and flasks of tea and coffee).

Although there was nobody else watching who was prepared to admit they could see, let alone talk to, either Bear (which they all agreed was a bit of a shame, and a bit of a surprise given the childlike qualities normally associated with lovers of the Summer Game), Reggie and Vivian found plenty to talk about (mostly arcane Bear stuff with which I will not bore you – but which Reggie found especially useful).

Michael and Robin had some interesting debates about past games, the England selectors, prospects for the upcoming Test and ODI Series and of course (this being England and the cricket season) the weather.

As it turned out they were also both alumni of the same grammar school as well – about 10 years apart!

As he explained to Reggie, this amused Vivian - because it made both Michael and Robin 'Old Edwardians' (the school was King Edward VI) and his Father's name was Edward.

The one thing that none of them talked about was work, so when they said goodbye at close of play, Reggie and Robin had no idea what Michael and Vivian did, nor why they were up in Town apparently doing it. And it mattered not one jot!

They did swap phone numbers though – and when they all declared that they would see each other again very soon they actually all meant it!

Oh yes, just to complete the perfect day they had all had, Devon (who Reggie and Robin were supporting because of their new friends) won the match by scrambling three runs off the very last ball – which made it the perfect end to the game too!

CHAPTER 6

Reginald Arbuthnot Cholmondeley woke up feeling as if he had been sprayed with an especially strong starch – he was stiff all over and as a consequence a tad grumpy! It undoubtedly didn't help his mood that he had been having an especially mouth-watering dream involving scones, some (well actually quite a lot!) of Robin's homemade jam and some (the same comment applies to this as to the jam) utterly delicious clotted cream. Unfortunately he had only got to the part where he had buttered, jammed and creamed a scone, he hadn't done the best bit – eating it!

He had fallen asleep on the sofa ("I really must stop doing that.") and had been roused by Lettie's usual response on Robin's return – total waggy pottiness!

Reggie could hear Robin in the Wheelhouse and thus, he was behind a closed door that the Dog couldn't open and get through no matter how hard she tried – but she was really, really giving it her best shot!

"Lettie," said Reggie sternly and in a general Dog direction.

At the sound of her name the Dog looked up, but, on realising that neither food nor walkies were in the offing, looked away almost at once and carried on bounding about for what she knew was Robin's imminent appearance. Unabashed, Reggie carried on, "It's all your fault that I got so tired out and dropped off." He was not in the best frame of mind and frankly, was looking for someone to blame for his physical and mental condition – and for the offence of interrupting his dream before he had been able to take so much as a single bite!

He cast his mind back to what had happened earlier in the day and how and why he had come to be so tired!

. . . . . . After their normal hearty breakfast (which had quickly become Reggie's favourite meal of the day – although Robin was far too fond of saying "Start the day off right with a good breakfast.") Robin had gone off to work.

It was an 'In the Office' day for Robin, so Reggie had stayed on the Boat), leaving Bear and Dog to look after each other – which was a regular occurrence and had not, up until today (as it turned out), been problematic.

Reginald Arbuthnot Cholmondeley had however, earmarked this particular day as the day on which he was going to take Lettie for a walk all on his own. By this he didn't mean just getting off the Boat and letting her wander around doing the stuff that Dogs do when they go walkies – what he had in mind was an actual *bona fide*, just like what Robin does, walk.

Today he was determined to prove to Robin (and to Lettie and himself) that he was quite capable of actually taking the Dog for a 'proper' walk.

By way of preparation (and because it was a good idea generally), he had been exercising, albeit surreptitiously as he was very aware of how ridiculous he looked when doing it.

So, when he was alone (Lettie didn't count for these, very specific, purposes) he would do press-ups, sit ups, squat thrusts (well more squat pushes to be honest – they were really hard!) and quite a lot of running (OK walking quicker than he normally did) on the spot.

Thinking about it candidly he came to the conclusion that maybe, in truth, 'attempt' was a better word than 'do' – but he sincerely felt he was getting better at them and consequently, getting fitter.

On the basis that positive reinforcement is a powerful tool he had told his body that it was now a finely tuned machine that was more than capable of, if not keeping up with the Dog (even the Boys with all their excess energy couldn't do that!), then at least moseying more than fifty yards from where the jetty met the shore!

Obviously his body made up its own mind (it wasn't entirely impressed and was certainly not convinced!) but, "Hey," it thought, "it isn't up to me, the brain is in command and can make me do stuff that I'm not really up for whether I like it or not." So that was that – today they (that is Reggie and his, frankly still dubious, body) were going to take Lettie for a proper walk – provided the weather was as nice as it was supposed to be. Walking was going to be quite enough of a trial without also getting wet – which was assuredly *not* on the agenda.

The first few times Reggie had taken her off the Boat for some middle of the day exercise he had put Lettie on her lead.

This was at Robin's suggestion, as the Dog understood (even if she didn't like it – which she didn't) that restraining her in that manner meant that she was to stay with you until the lead was taken off. The first time they did this didn't go entirely according to plan though as Reggie nearly got pulled into the water!

Lettie was used to having a human (adult or a child) on the other end and she hadn't factored in (or bluntly, cared much about) the fact that Reggie was nowhere near as strong as they were!

Luckily Reggie's instinct was to let go immediately (which saved him from a dunking!) and his desperate cries of "Come back here Lettie," (he was terrified she would run away) told the Dog that she had better return on the instant – which, much to Reggie's intense relief, she duly did!

Anyway, after three or four similar episodes, Reggie became resigned to trusting the Dog to do the right thing – and, thankfully she had done so, at least so far!

Lettie had gradually come to terms with what was expected of her – gauging by experimentation how much she could pull on the lead and then toning it down appropriately. There was still major bouncing and the inevitable manic wagginess but she stayed within a perimeter she considered acceptable (it just about was) and they established a routine that worked for them.

Reggie reckoned, with some justification, that he had mastered the standard task of giving Lettie a little exercise (and the opportunity to have a wee!) quite some time ago and accordingly, it was no longer a challenge.

Today was going to be different however, even though Lettie hadn't been made aware of this yet. They were going to leave the safety of the immediate vicinity of the Boat and boldly go where no Dog and Bear had gone before (yes, Reggie was a science fiction fan!). Actually the route was very well known to both of them – but just not doing it on their own; that is to say without Robin or the Boys.

The morning went past quite quickly. Reggie, as he usually did, meandered around the Boat generally tidying up (by now he actually felt he was entitled to refer to his efforts as 'shipshaping' – at least Robin was grateful for the hard(ish) work he put in.

About midday Reggie had a sandwich and a glass of milk for his lunch and after a suitable interval to let his digestive system deal with it ("It would be awful if I had to give up because I got cramp or a stitch.") he made up his mind that now was the time.

The die was cast!

"It'll be quite an adventure," Reggie said to Lettie, who he thought looked like she understood; but that could simply have been the normal show of enthusiasm which Lettie's inherent optimism triggered whenever anyone got off a chair and stood up – which the Bear had just done!

Reggie got the key for the padlock on the outer door (he quite often locked the door after Robin had left as he didn't want anyone he didn't know coming in unannounced).

Lettie knew exactly what this key was for and she pricked up her ears and started cautiously building up the potential for bounce and waggieness which would be unleashed if they *actually* went. When next the lead was taken down from the hook it lived on (Reggie always took the lead – just in case) Lettie knew that this was not a drill. This was her cue – she was off and heading for the door!

All the protestations in the world couldn't calm Lettie down at this point, so Reggie, in line with the protocol he had in his head for his little trips with the Dog off the Boat, didn't even bother trying. He calmly and methodically put the key in the lock, undid it, removed it and started sliding the door back.

Lettie was, by now, used to Reggie doing this and was as passive as she ever was (that is to say not at all!) when she was about to be allowed off the Boat to go nuts outside!

She still did the whole 'squeezing past' thing, but Reggie was ready for it and got out of the way to let her go. She was out the door and on the jetty before you could say 'perambulate' or even the much shorter 'walk'! She did show her grasp of the rules by staying on the jetty immediately by the Boat – but she was now very close to full on bounce/wag mode.

After he had closed and locked the door Reggie said, "Off you go then girlie."

And off she jolly well went!

Reggie walked very carefully as always, over the gangplank between the Boat and the jetty and noted that Lettie was sticking to no more than the accepted distance away from him.

He sighed, as he usually did, with utter relief at the fact that the Dog had not bolted and thought, as he also usually did, "Thank goodness she is such a good Dog, I have not even the glimmer of an idea as to how I would tell Robin I'd lost Lettie."

As he walked towards her Lettie bounded away, but she never went farther away than she was supposed to; almost as if she actually *was* on a lead – albeit a long one! This behaviour was repeated throughout the walk – although she did occasionally come right back up to where he was only to then rush off again! She was, as she always did, having a really *great* time.

This being the first occasion he had tried this experiment Reggie had decided to walk around the harbour – the same area he had been taken on the first time he had met the Boys. There were two reasons for this. First there were no roads, so no danger of Lettie having an accident, and secondly the sight of a dog pottering about (apparently alone to grown up eyes) in that area was much less likely to cause suspicion and/or some sort of action than if the same thing happened near traffic.

The walk was thankfully uneventful and thoroughly enjoyable – but by the time they got back to the Boat, Reggie was downright tuckered out. He was, he felt, less exhausted than he would have been had he not been working out – but he was still pooped. Lettie was still only on her second wind and, unsurprisingly, would have been quite happy to stay out for ages longer. For a first time though Reggie felt that, for him at least, they had been out for long enough – but he was mightily disappointed when he checked the clock and found that they had only been gone 30 minutes! "It seemed much longer," he mused as he sat on the edge of the Boat and brushed the dirt off his feet. He went back inside, deciding not to lock up this time as he expected Robin back quite early.

Then, having sorted out all the stuff that needed doing, Reggie got up on the sofa, opened his book – and, before he could read even a single page, promptly (and very deeply) fell asleep! . . . . . .

CHAPTER 7

So there was Reggie – stiff as a board from having indulged (actually over indulged!) in unaccustomed exercise and then falling asleep on the sofa in a less than correct postural attitude. One of the things that he had forgotten before deciding to undertake the walk was that he was still often carried on Robin's shoulders when they walked Lettie – so he was so not used to walking anything like the distance that he had walked that afternoon. "Note to self – think these things through much more thoroughly." That thought was too late to help him in his current predicament but he wasn't about to forget it in the future.

At this point Robin came into the Saloon. "Hi there chap and chappess. How are we all doing this beautiful evening then?" This was some way beyond even Robin's normal positive and cheerful demeanour – Reggie waited with bated breath for the particularly good news he knew must have precipitated this elevation in his Human's disposition.

Sure enough something 'completely brilliant' had happened that day to put Robin's 'jolliness factor' up quite a few notches.

"Guess what Reggie."

The Bear knew this to be a rhetorical question so he just waited for the rest of it, which came almost immediately!

"U Support was given a box for the day/night T20 international at the Rose Bowl tomorrow to raise some money by getting people to make a donation in exchange for getting to see the game. That was good news of course, but the thing is that two of the people that had already paid their donations can't make it now – and given the shortness of the notice they don't want their money back and I got the nod to go and to bring a friend. Obviously you can come anyway, but how about we ask Michael and Vivian if they can make it? I know it's really short notice but it has to be worth a shot, don't you think?"

At this news and at the possibility of seeing his new friends again so soon, all Reggie's stiffness was forgotten and his grumpy disposition vanished.

"I'll send Vivian a text right now," he said, and he got out the mobile phone (Robin had got him it for emergencies) and proceeded to compose his text.

GOT TCKT 4 GAME @ RB 2MOZ – CAN U & M MAKE IT? BIG SOZ IT SUCH SHRT NOTIS. RAC.

Reggie had had lessons from the Boys on texting. He hadn't got the hang of it yet, but he was getting better (or as Robin viewed the whole thing, worse!).
Robin put the kettle on and went into the Cabin to get changed.
"Goodness, that was quick. Great news, they can make it," shouted Reggie.
Robin came back into the Saloon and read the response.

BRILL. US IN TOWN, TO EXETER 2MO ANYWAY WILL DIVERT & MEET U AT GROUND. WOT TIME & WHERE? VIV

"Ask him if they need picking up from a train station, or if they're driving," said Robin. So Reggie sent back:

GET 2 RB BY 3.30. U IN CAR OR NEED PICKUP FROM STATION? RAC

Quick As a flash back came

IN CAR. TA THO. C U @ MAIN GATE @ 3.30 – OK? VIV

Before he sent a text back Reggie asked, "Is that OK Robin?"
Robin nodded.

COOL BEANS. CANT WAIT 2 C U BOTH. RAC

Vivian was obviously adept at the text thing as just as quickly as before, he came back with:

US 2 – C U 2 THERE. VIV

"So that's great isn't it – what shall we have for tea then?"

The next day Robin was working from home anyway, but nevertheless, because they were both so excited, the time just dragged really slowly until about 2.30 p.m., when, after having left Lettie with Barbara, Robin and Reggie boarded TW to make their way to the Rose Bowl for the match.

By way of explanation Robin had said, "We'll be taking the Bike for the usual reasons Reggie – traffic and parking."

That was fine with Reggie in any event – a trip on TW and a cricket match at the end of it – result!

The weather was perfect – clear skies and while not exactly warm, certainly not too cold. This did mean however, that it was likely to get quite parky later on when the sun went down.

Robin had made sure they had their fleeces, scarves, gloves and hats as a hedge against this.

"Don't forget," said Robin, "we're in a hospitality box, so we can always shelter in there if it gets too, too cold."

Bear and Human were long past the point in their relationship were there needed to be any quasi-macho posturing – so Reggie just said, "Good."

So there they were, making their way the short distance up the motorway to the home of Hampshire cricket, the Rose Bowl. They arrived in plenty of time to park TW and get over to the Main Entrance so that they wouldn't miss Michael and Vivian. Once again the ease with which Robin was able to find a parking space was further evidence of how great the Bike was. Robin didn't even need to avail himself of the services of his Parking Fairy!

At 3.25 Michael and Vivian hove into view. Robin waved and shouted, "Hi Guys, over here," to let them know where to come, as the crowd was big – and getting bigger by the minute.

The four friends exchanged greetings, Robin handed Michael his ticket and they all went into the ground.

Robin led the way to the box that U Support had been given.

When they got there, Robin and Reggie both said to Michael and Vivian respectively, "Can I take your coat?"

"Thank you, most kind," came the replies and off they came.

As both Michael and Vivian turned round to hand their coats to Robin and Reggie the former noticed something different about the attire of both their friends from the way they had been dressed at Lord's. They both had stiff white collars with no opening at the front – which Robin knew to be a distinctive symbol of members of the clergy.

"We had no idea that you were a Man and a Bear of the Cloth," said Robin.

He then noticed that both were also wearing purple shirts (although he knew that, officially, the colour is violet).

"Ah," he said, "I also see that you are both Bishops."

He paused, momentarily at a loss for words (unusual as that was and unlikely as it sounds) and then went on, "That must be, if I may say so, both fascinating and fulfilling –if occasionally frustrating."

Michael and Vivian exchanged a look – they were both used to their collars having an effect on people, and not always a positive one unfortunately.

Vivian said, "I do hope you don't think we were hiding our vocations from you when we met as nothing could be further from the truth."

Robin was shocked that they might even consider that he might have thought that and he said so.

Having been reassured on that point, Vivian went on, "We were in mufti, I know, but the subject never came up and frankly we were all having such a good time that it didn't seem to matter."

Which it most certainly does not," said Reginald Arbuthnot Cholmondeley, "any more than Robin being a lawyer matters." Robin looked shamefaced and the other three burst into peels of laughter – and Robin joined in.

Robin said to Michael, "Would I be right in thinking that Exeter is your diocese then? Should we address you as My Lord."

He looked a little embarrassed, because he was unsure if he was (or had previously been) crossing any protocol lines – albeit entirely inadvertently.

Michael replied, "That's right Robin. I am the Bishop of Exeter, and Vivian is the Ursine Bishop of Sherborne. While we are, as it were, 'collared up', you might call me Bishop Michael but I am happy for you and Reggie to continue to call me just Michael. It is really up to you." Vivian nodded in agreement.

Robin took a deep breath and then exhaled - banishing any concerns or nerves he may have had to simply vanish in the air.

"Excellent. Well then, Michael and Vivian it is – but I think I will introduce you to everyone as Bishop Michael, if that is the correct form."

Michael nodded to signify that he was cool with the suggested way forward. Robin felt that there was one more thing he needed to say, so he said, "Do please accept my apologies if I have in any way made either of you feel uncomfortable as a result of my awkwardness and stupidity."

"No problem Robin," said Vivian, "believe me we hear a lot worse than that all too regularly." He added, "I hope we are cool?" Robin nodded gratefully.

Robin couldn't help thinking that this was a very good example of the way that when someone thinks there might be an elephant in the room, issues that are of concern but which no one talks about (and in this case, it was really only Robin that thought there might be), they usually turn out to be imagined or easily resolved when addressed and openly discussed.

And with that all sorted they got on with the serious business of the day – having a good time and watching the cricket.

Robin introduced Michael to Adam, the Founder of the Charity he worked for – U Support. Pretty soon the two of them became engrossed in a conversation about the work U Support was involved in and Robin decided to leave them to it and to go and get a drink – he felt that he deserved one as he had made a complete and utter twerp of himself!

He had learned an important truth which he had believed he had known already, that it's the people, not the job (or anything else external) and that making snap judgements (even unconsciously as he had done) about people based on incomplete information often causes the drawing of incorrect and potentially offensive conclusions. "You would have thought that meeting Reggie would have taught me that." He said to himself.

By now he had reached the drinks table. Ignoring the alcohol he went instead for a cup of strong, black coffee as he was riding TW after all. Even though he didn't have to ride again for eight hours, he was not happy that his system would have got rid of any alcohol he might have had by the time he got back on the Bike – and he knew that the only safe way to drink and drive is *not* to drink anything alcoholic at all!

Meanwhile the Bears had made their way to the buffet table and were avidly discussing the relative merits of cheese with or without pickle – and whether brown or yellow pickle was best!

Clearly a deep and meaningful discussion!

Just about then there was a burst of applause from the crowd – the captains were on the way out to the middle for the toss.

Everyone stopped what they were doing to watch. England won and chose to field first – game on!

There was still time for everyone to get a drink and some food and make themselves comfortable before the players took the field – the England team to field and the opposition batsmen to face the England bowling attack.

Robin and Reggie, Michael and Vivian sat down with plates and cups. They all had soft drinks as Bears aren't keen on alcohol and Michael was driving back to Exeter after the game and he shared Robin's view on drinking and driving!

As there was still a little time before the game started Vivian asked Reggie to tell him a little more about his background, "As we seem to have managed to assuaged any concerns Robin had about discussing personal matters." He said this with a distinct twinkle in his eye and with his tongue firmly in his cheek!

Robin, who had noticed both, raised his eyes skyward and said, "You got me Vivian – what penance do I need to serve?" This was clearly said in the same spirit, so they all laughed!

"Well," said Vivian, using his best Bishop's voice, "Penance is meant to teach, not to punish and it seems to me that you have already learned a valuable truth today. I do feel however, that it may be appropriate to reinforce the lesson. I suggest that you act as drinks monitor for the three of us for the duration of the game – does that sound fair?"

Both Michael and he adopted sombre and serious looks and Michael said, "Good idea." Regrettably this attempt to wind Robin up lost all its impact as after a few seconds they both almost dissolved in a fit of the giggles!

Notwithstanding the obvious implication that neither of them considered penance necessary, Robin was still painfully aware that he had behaved wrongly so he said, "It's very kind of you both to be so generous at my failings – but I am happy to act as *sommelier* for the day, even though we are none of us drinking wine!"

More laughter all round!

"So, Reggie, tell Michael and me about yourself."

"Gosh, well, where to start."

Reginald Arbuthnot Cholmondeley was having the same sort of feelings of mild embarrassment that he had experienced when he first explained his antecedents to Robin.

"Deep breath Reginald," he told himself, "No need for false modesty or, much worse, exaggeration."

Before he could begin his tale however, Robin (who recognised Reggie's dilemma and wanted to give him time to gather his thoughts) said, "Can we do that in a minute, please. Vivian, I am fascinated as to how you can be Bishop of Sherborne. I know that the Diocese of Sherborne was created in about 705 and that it had the Diocese of Crediton (to cover Devon and Cornwall) carved out of it in 909. But I thought that it got moved to Old Sarum and was then moved again in 1227 when it became the Diocese of Salisbury – which it remains. So how can you be Bishop of it now?"

Reginald Arbuthnot Cholmondeley had somehow contrived to look both grateful and also mildly annoyed at Robin's interruption (especially as he had just summoned up the courage to actually tell his story) – but now he looked astonished at his friend's display of knowledge of ecclesiastical annals. Michael and Vivian both looked equally amazed.

"Well," said Robin (who had recovered his normal *sang froid* and was secretly pleased at their reactions), "I wasn't always a lawyer you know. I have a History degree and I remember all that from my studies is all!" Inwardly he was thinking, "Gotcha!" A bit unworthy of him perhaps but quite funny all the same.

Vivian recovered his equilibrium first – it was his Diocese they were discussing after all, "I am impressed Robin. Frankly I am not convinced that many clerics would know that!" Michael nodded and smiled – at which Robin (who still had some residual unease about his earlier stupidity) was relieved and pleased to see. Reginald Arbuthnot Cholmondeley still looked astonished but at least he had closed his mouth now!

"You are right Robin about the original Diocese of Sherborne, and what happened to it. What you clearly didn't know, and there is no reason why you should have done, is that it was a joint Ursine/Human Diocese when it was originally created – and for a long time the Bear Bishop co-existed with the Human one. Indeed it was often the case that the Ursine Bishop managed to get his own Human selected as the corresponding Human Bishop. For a long time now though (centuries in fact) the Diocese has been exclusively for Bears and, as such, I have the responsibility for the pastoral care of Bears in Devon and Cornwall and much of Wiltshire and Dorset; basically the areas covered by the Human Dioceses of Salisbury and Exeter. I share Michael's seat of the Cathedral Church of Saint Peter in Exeter, which is very convenient for both of us of course."

While his friend was explaining the ins and outs of the history of his Diocese Reggie was trying to imagine what Vivian would look like in his full Bishop's attire.

Frankly his ideas were a bit short on detail – but he knew that Vivian would look very smart and both approachable and authoritative.

"Right. Well that all makes perfect sense given what I have come to know about the importance of Bears in the history of England since I met Reggie," said Robin.

Robin had the germ of an idea but as it involved asking his friends a pretty big (well he thought it was big) favour he wasn't sure how to broach the subject just yet, so he kept quiet – until a suitable opportunity presented itself.

"As I saying before I was not at all rudely, interrupted." Reginald Arbuthnot Cholmondeley wanted to get back to his tale – before he lost his bottle! "Not that the history lesson wasn't interesting, because of course it was."

He was clearly still floundering and in imminent danger of losing the plot.

Vivian recognised this and before Reggie could continue his descent into incoherence said, "No, please go on Reggie do tell Michael and I your story. I don't know of any Bear that doesn't have one – and they are always intriguing and certainly worth hearing."

As Vivian (who was an even more perceptive Bear than Reginald Arbuthnot Cholmondeley) had known it would this strengthened Reggie's confidence sufficiently to help him start his account.

"Well," Reginald Arbuthnot Cholmondeley began telling his tale much as he had when he told Robin but with lots of stuff that he now, after exposure to Robin and the Boys, considered to be a little boastful and which should as a consequence be left out.

When he had finished Vivian looked at Michael and on getting a positive nod said, "We can help you with your problem Reggie."

Just then the crowd started cheering as England came out onto the field with their opponent's opening batsmen following shortly after – at which point their supporters (of which there were a lot) added to the general volume of noise reverberating round the ground.

Michael, Vivian, Robin and even Reggie temporarily forgot their conversation to join in with the common excitement!

Eventually things settled down and England's opening bowler started down the track to bowl the first ball – game on!

It was a scorcher, very fast and straight, that went directly through the batsman's defence and took his middle stump out of the ground!

The English crowd (including the four friends) went crazy!

While the batsman trudged dejectedly back to the dressing room, Vivian came back to his train of thought. "Both Michael and I sit in the House of Lords Reginald and we know the people who hold the Offices of State, some personally and others only by reputation. In this case I think the Lord Great Chamberlain is the appropriate person to talk to. What do you think Michael?"

Michael replied, "Certainly Vivian – and as you are aware I know the family, so I am sure we could get Reginald an early appointment."

Both of them understood that this was a very serious matter, which probably explains why they were both using Reggie's full first name.

Reginald Arbuthnot Cholmondeley was utterly speechless – a state almost unheard of for him!

Michael said, "The Lord Great Chamberlain is responsible for Royal affairs in the Palace of Westminster and has jurisdiction for areas of the Palace not administered by the Commons or Lords. The current holder of the Office, and I suspect you didn't know this, is David Cholmondeley 7th Marquess of Cholmondeley – so he is almost certainly a distant relative of yours!"

As if this wasn't massive enough news Vivian then provided the *coup de grace*, "AND I know his Bear, George Hugh Malpas, also probably a long-lost cousin of your family, who works with his Human in the House of Lords."

This, frankly astounding and brilliant news was just too much for Reggie who reacted by coughing and spluttering (though not necessarily in that order).

The only word anyone could recognise him saying was "Wow!" – but that actually summed up his feelings perfectly!

Robin was also elated. First for his friend, naturally, and secondly because his idea was to ask Michael and/or Vivian to get Reggie and him an appointment with the appropriate person at the House of Lords. Now, because they had offered, he didn't even have to ask – which, in all honesty, he was relieved about. Plus the fact that the appropriate person had his own Bear (he briefly forgot that it is the other way round!) and they were both possibly relatives of *his* Bear (albeit a long way back) meant they would already have an insight into Reggie's family history.

What an absolutely stonking result!

Meanwhile Vivian was patting Reggie on the back, suggesting that he "take deep breaths old chap," and Michael was offering him a drink.

Eventually Reggie calmed down enough to remember his manners and say, "That would be so very kind of you if it wouldn't be too much trouble?"

Both Michael and Vivian assured him that it wouldn't be any trouble at all and that they would be more than happy to arrange a meeting as soon as possible.

"Righty ho then that's sorted." Reggie sounded much more calm than he actually felt, "Back to the important stuff then – the cricket."

The other three understood that Reggie was trying to be play down the importance to him of what had just happened, and they all went along with his wishes.

By now the opposition's number three batsman was taking guard at the crease so the four friends by mutual if unspoken consent left the matter of restoring Reginald Arbuthnot Cholmondeley to his name and title on the back burner (where Reggie had put it) and settled down to the important business at hand - watching the game.

And what a corker it was!

England won with a six hit halfway through the last over, but not before giving their fans some anxious moments first.

Having looked like they were going to cruise to victory the England team suffered their almost customary middle order batting collapse before scampering home at the end!

All in all though the match was much enjoyed by everyone, and U Support made a very acceptable amount of money for charity – another great result!

CHAPTER 8

Reginald Arbuthnot Cholmondeley woke up in his bed on the Boat. It was peaceful and quiet, with only the sounds of the harbour floating in the air. The gently lapping waves against the side of the Boat, the occasional call of a water bird and the relaxing beating of his heart in his right ear as it pressed into his pillow!

He came fully awake feeling quite rested and serene but then he remembered what day it was, and everything changed. His heart began racing, his paws became clammy and he felt a little nauseous.

"Oh dear, today's *the* day, isn't it?"

With a dread sense of an inevitable and impending doom he peered out of the covers and looked at the calendar. Yes, he was right, today *was* the day – the day of his appointment with the Lord Great Chamberlain (and his Bear) at the House of Lords.

Robin poked his head around the door, "Morning Reginald old Bear. How the deuce are we this extremely fine and fair good morning?"

"What! How on earth can you be so wretchedly cheerful and jolly; have you totally lost your marbles; have your wits run off and joined the Foreign Legion; has your brain turned to mush?" Running out of colourful images he resorted to more a direct question, laced with an insult, "Buffoon, have you no idea what day it is today?"

In response Robin was coolness personified, "Relax Reggie. I know that today is the day we go to see the Human and the Bear, probably your long-lost cousins, who, once they recognise you for who you really are, are going to be able to do the necessary to restore your name and title – so why all the negative vibes?"

"But what if they don't acknowledge me for who I really am? What happens then?" Reginald Arbuthnot Cholmondeley was having a panic attack – and the sun was only just coming up, so not a good start to the day.

"Look here, dummy," Robin had experience of dealing with this sort of thing and he chose the 'shock tactics' route, "this is going to work you idiot. George Malpas and his Human, Lord Cholmondeley, *are* going to accept your credentials, and acknowledge that you are who you are and by later on this afternoon you will be so embarrassed by your little outburst that you will want to curl up and die rather than celebrate, *capice*!"

"But..." Reggie was weakening.

"But me no buts you spineless toad, out of that pit and give me twenty." They'd watched a war film the night before and that was a direct quote from when the heroes were in training!

Reggie couldn't be miserable or even cross at this so he just started laughing like the proverbial drain instead.

Robin breathed a huge sigh of relief. He had been worried that the last bit might have been about three steps too far but it had worked and Reggie was out of the dumpy doldrums and back on his true form – result!

"Sorry Robin. I had a bit of a funny five minutes there. *Pax*?"

"Of course, doofus." Robin was so relieved at the change he had helped effect he didn't take advantage of the situation to have a little fun with the Bear.

"Right then now that that's dealt with, how about breakfast? Start the day off right with a good breakfast that's what I always say."

At this umpteenth repetition of one of Robin's favourite phrases Reggie felt comforted and he laughed with the sheer joy of it all. Robin honestly had no idea why but he let it pass cos his friend was obviously totally out of his bad mood and that was what he had hoped for.

It was only two days after the match at the Rose Bowl that Vivian had phoned with the great news that Michael had arranged an appointment with Lord Cholmondeley at the House of Lords.

Today was the day of the appointment (if Reggie's manic outburst hadn't already given that away) and so after walking Lettie, doing their ablutions and having breakfast they got into the Car (with the Dog) and started off on their journey. They were both smartly suited and booted – well they were going to the Mother of Parliaments, which merited dressing up out of respect if nothing else. Luckily Barbara had finished Reggie's suit (and very chic he looked in it too) and this was its very first outing – which couldn't be either more appropriate or a better omen.

They dropped Lettie off at Barbara's house and off they went towards Reginald Arbuthnot Cholmondeley's destiny!

Robin had decided that it would be best if they took the train, so they parked in the station car park at Southampton Parkway and got on the express to Waterloo. An hour later they were in the great metropolis.

It was only a short tube ride from Waterloo to Westminster. To be fair Reggie was not entirely enamoured of the underground – it was labyrinthine, smelly and claustrophobic and generally not favourably inclined towards Bears.

In fact at one point Robin had to carry Reggie as it was so crowded that the adults using it, who would normally have steered round the Bear whilst wondering what they were avoiding, kept barging into him – and not even apologising when they did so! "That is just outright rudeness, but who can be surprised that people act like animals when they are treated as such," was Reggie's comment on the whole entirely regrettable if necessary experience.

Reggie was glad they only had to travel one stop.

Robin didn't have the heart to tell his friend that the Jubilee Line was really quite new and that some other parts of the system were over one hundred years old – and were showing their age.

He also didn't think that now was a good time to point out that he had used the tube every morning and evening (a trip of more than an hour each way) when he had worked in the West End, as he understood that Reggie needed all his focus on the meeting they were going to.

They came out of the underground and walked the short distance past Boadicea's statue, along Bridge Street, into Parliament Square, past the Palace of Westminster to its St. Stephen's Entrance.

Robin made himself known to the policeman on duty and explained that he had an appointment with Lord Cholmondeley, whereupon he was passed through to the security guards inside. He produced identification (his driving licence) and had his photograph taken to go on his Visitor's Pass.

To the astonishment of both Robin and Reggie the guard turned to the latter, "Good morning sir. You must be Reginald Arbuthnot Cholmondeley."

"Um, yes I am," replied the astonished Bear. He decided that not asking questions about how or why the guard could see him was probably the best policy.

"Please stand on this stool if you would be so kind. It's so that we can take your picture for the Pass." Reggie did as requested and his Pass was duly produced and handed to him to put round his neck (it was laminated and on a black cord).

"If you would be so good as to go to that window and tell the lady there who you have come to see. She'll organise things for you." And with that he smiled and saluted.

Reggie and Robin were both pleasantly surprised and impressed by the polite capability that the unpleasant but necessary task of ensuring the safety of Parliament was dealt with.

It was also *definitely* a good omen that he had spelt Reggie's name correctly!

The lady at the window was equally polite and efficient. She took their names, checked one of her many lists, made a phone call and asked them to, "Please take a seat over there," explaining that, "An Usher will be along shortly to conduct you to the Lord Great Chamberlain's office."

In no time at all another member of the Palace staff arrived and asked if they would please be good enough to accompany him.

So off they went.

They were guided through corridors, up stairs and past so many rooms that they lost count of how many there were until they arrived at a door marked 'Lord Great Chamberlain'.

They had arrived!

The Usher knocked on the door and opened it when he heard "Please do come in," from inside.

He announced them to the man behind the desk facing the door, "Robin Goddard and Reginald Cholmondeley, to see his Lordship."

"Thank you. I'll take them in," said the man behind the desk who was the Lord Great Chamberlain's Clerk (there was a plaque on the desk identifying him as such).

With that their guide left – Robin just managing to say "Thank you," in his general direction before he got out of the door!

Robin turned back round as the Clerk was knocking on the door to the Lord Great Chamberlain's actual office.

"Come in please."

The door was opened and, with a gesture from the Clerk that they should, they walked through.

This was it!

170

Robin's first impression of the office was that it was large enough to be comfortable but not so big as to be showy or aggressive – and it was definitely well used! The best term to use would be 'organised chaos', with the emphasis on the word 'organised' (meaning that the chaos was well understood by the person or people who had created it).

Before Reggie and Robin had the chance to feel stressed (well any *more* stressed than they already were!) a tall, very smartly dressed Bear came round from behind the desk and said, "We are so very pleased to meet you both. I am George Hugh Malpas and the chap over there is David Cholmondeley, my Human," he giggled in an utterly charming way and went on, "and for his sins, he is the Lord Great Chamberlain."

He extended his right paw towards Reggie and went on, "You are obviously Reginald Cholmondeley. There is simply no mistaking you. I knew your Father quite well and I must say that the family resemblance is almost uncanny."

Reggie took the proffered paw and shook it.

He was desperately trying to process what was happening but luckily his upbringing came to his rescue (although it was done on some form of automatic politeness pilot) and he said, "How do you do. Yes, I am indeed Reginald Arbuthnot Cholmondeley. Thank you for recognising me as such."

Meanwhile the two Humans had introduced themselves and shaken hands.

They then swapped over – with each Bear formally introducing himself to each Human, and *vice-versa*.

Formalities over and Robin and Reggie having been told to use David and George rather than titles and the like they all sat down in the chairs indicated and the most pressing question was asked – did they want tea or coffee, and would they like biscuits or some homemade fruitcake ("from our place in Norfolk," said David, "do try some, it's scrumptious.").

Reggie and Robin both plumped for tea and fruitcake.

"So let's deal with the business at hand shall we?" George said, "Bishop Vivian has told me your tale as you explained it to him and in all the circumstances I don't see that there is any problem, do you David?"

George's Human shook his head, "No George. I think we can safely say that as you have been satisfied with Reggie's *bona fides* as his Father's son means that we can sort the necessary paperwork and get his name and title back where it belongs, namely with him. I shouldn't think it'll take very long either."

Reggie exchanged a delighted (and relieved) glance with Robin – what an absolutely cracking result!

"What can I say," said Reginald Arbuthnot Cholmondeley, "except a heartfelt huge thank you."

And that really was all that needed to be said.

They all had a very pleasant chat about lots of things, everything and nothing. Robin and David had a mutual interest in film and talked about some quite obscure stuff. George and Reggie talked Bears – especially the uniqueness of Reggie's situation in having got an adult Human.

As it turned out George had inherited David from his (that is George's) Father, much as Vivian had taken on Michael from his Father. It appeared that this was quite normal in the Bear world. Reggie thought about Robin's Boys. He looked forward to the time his children took them on if that was to be the way it happened, which he earnestly hoped it would be. It was, but that is another story.

"One thing I found strange George, was that the staff could see me – are they not grown up?" This question had been playing on Reggie's mind.

"No, they are a bit of an anomaly in that they notice us Bears, but not really as Bears. You see you and I are not the only Bears who have access to, and use, the Palace. I have always presumed that the staff receive some form of special Bear training, but I am so used to it I don't notice it anymore."

Eventually, to the regret of all four, Reggie and Robin had to go. They had taken up quite enough of George and David's valuable time and they both had work to do.

As they left George said to Reggie, "Now don't worry about a thing. We'll make sure all the relevant checks and paperwork get done. Rest assured we will be seeing each other again soon – when you take your seat." He said it with such confidence that Reggie actually *did* stop worrying.

Reginald Arbuthnot Cholmondeley felt simply wonderful (as well as much relieved). He had fulfilled the promise he had made his Father, and could start to get on with the rest of his life as a Bear living on a Boat!

The journey home was uneventful and pretty much made in silence as both Reggie and Robin considered the implications of the day's events.

After putting the Car away Robin and Reggie walked into the town (Reggie on Robin's shoulders) and picked up Lettie. She was her normal potty, waggy self and her influence helped to break the spell and bring them both back down to earth.

The walk had been Robin's idea, "Let's get us a bit of fresh air shall we?" Reggie had nodded his assent – he needed some!

Reggie was the first to speak – but only just! "I do hope this won't change things Robin because I really love living here with you and the Boys."

Robin smiled a huge smile – 'nuff said!

"I thought we might take a trip with Alex and Ian on the Boat. Nothing special just up and down the coast a bit, maybe take a week or so to just chill. What do you think?"

Before Reggie could answer Robin added, "My Lord," and bowed. The response of Reginald Arbuthnot Cholmondeley, 9th Viscount of the Salop Oak to the use of his title was to throw a cushion, which missed!

They both laughed with the sheer joy of that moment and with anticipation for all the moments yet to come – and Lettie got waggier.

"That sounds like a great idea Robin – let's do it."

And that was exactly what they did.

Thank you for reading our Book. We all hope you really enjoyed it.

Robin Goddard, June Trafford and

This Book is raising money for:

It's not just a charity...

By buying this Special Limited Edition of A Very English Bear you have made a substantial contribution to a very worthy cause – U Support – because we (the author, illustrator and publisher) have given the Charity the right to __all__ the proceeds of its sales.

*Here is a message from the Chairman and Co-Founder of U Support. **Please** read it.*

U Support is a registered charity which purchases tickets for disabled, disadvantaged and deprived young people, together with those suffering from life limiting illnesses to attend sporting, cultural and leisure events. The tickets are then provided free of charge to the child and their carer.

Disabled children feel, often justifiably, that many places and activities are hard for them to access, which stops them from doing the things that other children and young people do. They want places where they can go to spend time with their friends, where they can feel included and just simply enjoy themselves.   Children are children, regardless of whether or not they have a disability, and parents recognize that involvement in sporting events will benefit their child in the same way as it does non-disabled children.

U Support also aims to generate awareness of the issues faced by those with hardship and to promote inclusivity demonstrating that disability or illness should not preclude kids from being kids.

U Support believes it is important that children have all different kinds of experiences. Every community should actively support and encourage the integration of individuals with disabilities, and these individuals should be encouraged to participate fully in the activities of our society.

In the UK, there are 770,000 disabled children under the age of 16 – which equates to one child in 20. Research shows that it costs up to three times as much to raise a disabled child, as it does to raise a child without disabilities. Statistics also show that 55% of families with a disabled child live in poverty, while 84% are in debt. Families may already feel the financial crunch from medical bills, medical equipment costs, prescriptions and transport expenses, therefore opportunities for recreation and leisure activities are limited. U Support is trying to redress the balance.

Beginning in 2003, and registered as a charity in 2009, U Support was founded by disabled entrepreneur Adam Gregory and his wife Tracey, both of whom had experienced first hand not only the difficulties faced by disabled young people but also the unbridled joy attending these events can bring.

Since 2003, U Support has purchased over 10,000 football tickets, but understanding not everyone enjoys football, extended the offering to pop concerts, and leisure activities providing the opportunity for young people to go to Disneyland Paris and to meet music stars such as JLS, Olly Murs, Take That and Adele.

Hardship and illness crosses international barriers too and in 2010 U Support extended its work to South Africa working with an children's AIDS orphanage and surrounding community, with the objective, subject to the receipt of funds, of assisting the community in becoming self sustainable rather than the 95% unemployment, no food, no clean water and no opportunities that currently exist.

Above all, whether at home or abroad, whether sports related, music, leisure or humanitarian, U Support needs YOUR support to continue and to achieve further and wider objectives, Of every pound received, not less than 90% is spent providing the opportunities you see.

To add your support or donation, please visit **www.usupport.org.uk** or contact : **U Support, 23-25 Portland Terrace, Southampton SO14 7EN**

Many thanks on behalf of myself and my fellow trustees.
Adam Gregory, Chairman & Co-Founder
U Support – Charity registration number 1128870